CRAZY IS AS CRAZY DOES

Part 1

A novella

Eva S. Pinkney

Cover design by Demont Pinder
First Edition

ISBN: 154516617X
ISBN 13: 9781545166178
Library of Congress Control Number: 2017906551
CreateSpace Independent Publishing Platform
North Charleston, South Carolina

To Mommy and Daddy, looking down from above: thank you for showing me what unconditional love means.
To my family, extended family, and friends: thank you for the love and support. I couldn't have done this without you.
To my two beautiful daughters, Raquel and Nikki: thank you for putting up with me.
To Jada and Chase: thank you for being my inspiration to make this transformation.
To my baby: thank you for being my rock. I will continue to be your ride or die.

Cover image by Demont "Peekaso" Pinder, www.demontpinder.com
Back cover photo by Kidada Kendall, kidadankkendall.com
Makeup by Arica Peni, AlreadyPerfectArtistry.com
Nails by V Spa & Nail Studio by KV & Jimmy, www.facebook.com/
vspa.nail.studio
Editing by Kayode Kendall, kayode.kendall@gmail.com

1

Fall 1987—Washington, DC

"**D**o Me Baby" blared loudly as I struggled with Fats's dry cleaning. The weight of the clothing was killing my arm. The sound of metal on wood, followed by a foot slowly being dragged, could be heard from the apartment across the hall. I wasn't trying to have no conversation with that nosy bitch. My right arm was numb. I quickly stuck the key in the lock, pulled the door toward me, and turned the key in the cylinder, hoping to dodge her ass.

"I need to have a word with you," the old lady said sternly, swinging her door open wide. The smell of ham hocks, collard greens, and pig feet cooking on the stove bum-rushed the hallway and lingered in the air like cheap perfume.

"Damn, too late," I muttered under my breath, rolling my eyes upward. I slowly turned to face her. Wiry strands of gray escaped from her receding hairline, and an outdated pair of spectacles, cracked in the corner, rested firmly on the tip of her nose and forced the hair to lick at the outside of her nostrils. A patch as bald as a baby's ass was quite evident at her temple—probably alopecia. One gold hoop earring held on to a badly split piercing. It hurt me to look. She removed her glasses and held them up to the sunlight, revealing sweaty armpits and flab, as she wiped the lenses with a used tissue from her pocket and then dabbed at the sweat on her forehead. Her puffy red face showed indentation marks from her apparent weight gain. She was wearing the same faded, funky-ass flowered housedress with the grease spot on the front as the first time we crossed paths. The material, snug to say the least, pulled at the seam, threatening to tear at any given moment, and pinned her sagging breasts to her three stomachs like a set of deflated balloons.

Mommy was all up in my head. "Amber, you respect your elders," she would say while cussing the shit out of a neighbor in the same breath.

"Yes, ma'am," I answered, looking the old lady square in the eye.

"Tell that boy to turn that music down. Disrespectful bastard. I knocked on that door thirty minutes ago. He never answered," she said, scratching unconsciously at the eczema on her arms and face as she spoke. "Hard as shit for me to get around on this walker. I don't like taking unnecessary steps. Understand me." Her words were more of a command than a question.

I glared at her fat ass as she pulled a silver flask from her left pocket, unscrewed the top, and took a long, hard swig. It wasn't even noon yet, and girlfriend was getting her drink on.

"I'll be sure to tell him," I said as I wrestled to shift the clothing to the other arm, wriggling my hand.

"Yip. Yip. Yip. Yip."

I looked back over my shoulder at the half dog, half rat making quite a racket while darting in and out from between legs the size of small tree trunks.

"Does he bite?" I asked as the Chihuahua inched closer, nipped at my ankles, and raced back to safety underneath her housedress.

"Only folks he don't like," the old lady said with a wide grin, proudly displaying a scattering of decayed teeth. "Shut it up, Bones."

The dog cowered, whimpering at the sound of her voice. He disappeared into the apartment with his tail tucked between his legs.

She never took her eyes off me as she backed her way into the open doorway, looking me up and down like I'd stolen something.

"It's saddidy bitches like you that make it hard for the rest of us, taking folks' men just for fun," she said with a snarl.

"Excuse me!" I said with much attitude.

"One of your kind took my husband. You half-cracker, loose-pussy, whoremongering bitch!" She hurled the insults at me like a barrage of icy snowballs finding their mark and then slammed the door in my face.

Flushed, I took a deep breath, turned, and pushed the apartment door open. The smell of boat was stagnant in the air. It hit my nostrils as soon as I crossed the doorsill. I walked straight to the sofa, dropped my purse, and laid the clothes down, smoothing out the Versace shirt on top through the plastic. Glancing up at the walls, I smiled, admiring several of Fats's paintings, thinking he was indeed gifted. I headed toward the bedroom; I was going to give Fats a piece of my mind. He promised me he wouldn't fuck with that shit no more, because he always did stupid shit when he was high on that boat.

A woman's moan wavered high over Prince on the stereo. I froze midstep. Fear ran through my veins as if I'd been struck by a bolt of lightning, with no warning. My feet were weighted down as if quick-dry cement had been poured all around me.

I had to see what I could smell—raw sex. Straight-up, hard-core fucking. My mind raced. Maybe it was one of Fats's workers with a stray hood rat from the avenue. I turned to leave, but a gnawing in my gut just wouldn't let me. I leaned in close to the wall, taking a chance on being seen or getting my head blown clean off. Everyone in Fats's crew was strapped twenty-four seven. I peeped around the corner.

"That's right! Just like that. Don't move. I got this," the woman said seductively.

Agile as a cat, she straddled Fats with both feet planted firmly on the mattress for leverage. The room was dim, but I could clearly see the contrast of their naked bodies, like black-and-white print on a newspaper. While squeezing her nipple with one hand, she gently massaged his balls with the other. The hair on his chest and legs, wet with perspiration, lay close like silk on an ear of sweet yellow corn as she repeatedly did squats on his dick, pussy juice gushing, running freely down his shaft like melted wax on a candle.

"I'm coming," she said softly and slowly as he grasped her around the waist. Fats had a way of making pussy purr. I knew this all too well.

The room was spinning. I grabbed the top of my head so it wouldn't explode. I knew that voice.

I peered into the room again. Her head was thrashing from left to right, like a fish out of water, swinging that coarse black horsehair, which hung to the crack of her ass, like she was in a Farrah Fawcett commercial. My suspicions were confirmed as I saw the caged bird take flight. Not even the small beads of sweat dampening its fragile wings could slow it down. It only gained momentum as I watched the tattoo just above her spine come to life. It was Chloe.

My heart sank. I clutched my chest. I needed air. Feelings of hurt, betrayal, and rage rose to the base of my throat like thick green bile. I swallowed hard as the tears burned my cheeks. The palms of my hands were sweaty, cutting away the lifeline that joined Chloe and I at the hip, like Siamese twins.

"Whip her motherfucking ass!" a voice said. "Jump on that bitch, and snatch that weave out from the root."

No. No.

"They both need to die," another voice said.

Listening to the voices, I headed for the kitchen and grabbed a butcher knife from the drawer. I was going to carve that skank a new asshole and cut his fucking heart out. In route to the bedroom, the knife raised in midair, and ready to strike, I stopped. The Lord truly must've intervened. What was I thinking? I wanted to accomplish too much with my life, and I damn sure wasn't about to spend the rest of it behind bars fighting off dike bitches on a daily.

I lowered the knife to my side, walked to the kitchen, and returned it to the drawer. I picked up my purse from the couch, gripping the leather shoulder straps tightly as I walked toward the door. I left and never looked back, thinking karma is a bitch with a way of sneaking up behind you and biting you in the ass when you least expect it.

My feet had barely touched the second step of the staircase when I thought about the old lady. I spun around and walked up to her apartment door. Knock, knock, knock. I ducked to the side, out of range of the peephole, hoping the fat bitch would just open the door. Metal on wood, a foot slowly being dragged.

"Who is it?" she yelled from the other side of the door.

I waited until I heard her fat clammy hands turn the lock. As soon as she opened the door, I sprang and pushed her fat ass hard. She landed with a loud thud, and the metal walker pinned her down. She lay floundering on the wooden floor, taking short gasping breaths, her face swollen like a blowfish.

"That's for every red woman you've disrespected without even knowing them! Fuck you!" I screamed while making my escape down the stairs and out the front door.

Mommy said be respectful of my elders, but only if they were respectful to me.

2

I opened my eyes, blinked rapidly, and finally let go of the remote I was still clasping in my hand. I tried to adjust to the stream of filtered light coming through the blinds of the floor-to-ceiling windows. It bounced off the five-carat diamond ring Fats bought the week before in Boca Raton. Wrenching, I turned away from the spectrum of light and twisted the rock to the inside of my finger. Its brilliance was blinding and too much to bear.

I attempted to sit up and tasted the drain trickle down my throat, an instant reminder of the night before. That shit was so good my mouth was still numb. Laying in wait, sending a subtle message.

"Aw shit." I grabbed my head with both hands, closed my eyes, and held on tight, as if that alone would stop the pounding. Every sound made the pain far worse. Tick. Tick. Tick. The second hand on the wall clock kept time with the carotid artery boldly pulsating on the side of my neck. My heart threatened to bust through my chest. Not even the ten milligrams of valium I swallowed with tap water sometime between 4:00 and 5:00 a.m. had calmed it down. I heard sparrows chirping just outside the bedroom window and the annoying buzz of a fly circling over the trash that was filled with vomit. The leaky toilet dripped—meant to get that shit fixed weeks ago. Now I was really paying for it.

I took a deep breath and exhaled. The smell of cognac escaped through partially opened lips. "Damn," I said, fanning my hand in front of my mouth to push away the fumes. Smoldering ash rose from the fireplace. The queasiness in my stomach returned.

My body felt constricted as if a giant anaconda was wrapped between my legs and curled around my rib cage, squeezing the life out of me. Reaching down between my legs, I snatched off the black lace thong that had been holding my clitoris hostage and unsnapped the harness that supported my thirty-four-triple-D tits, an unwanted gift from Mommy. I felt like shit warmed over.

"What the hell," I said, staring down at my hand, brushing crumbs of cocaine from my face, arms and legs. "I don't believe this shit. Must've fallen asleep with the package in my hand." My voice was low and cracked. I glanced around at the six empty Heineken bottles scattered on the nightstand next to the diamond-faced Cartier watch. Crumpled sheets of personalized powder blue stationery were strewn on the floor along with a blue Mont Blanc pen from when I had to get my feelings down on paper and then tossed that shit away, trying to get that hurt up off of me. So why didn't I feel any better?

Reaching over with a limp arm, I swatted at the bottom dresser drawer on the right-hand side, left ajar, filled with pleasurable toys. Fats was especially fond of the anal beads, hot oils, flavored condoms, and Fredrick's of Hollywood boobs-exposed ass-out gear, just for tricks. That's also where I keep the 9mm Fats gave me for protection.

"Let a motherfucker try to come up in this camp," I said with a smirk. "I got something for that ass."

The sound of footsteps crossing the marble foyer, moving further away, made me sit up. I grimaced at the pounding in my head and the cold, sticky substance underneath my hand; wet puke clung between my fingers like a webbing. I groaned. My body trembled as I wiped my hand on the sheet, not wanting to look.

An empty fifth of Remy rolled off the mattress, hit the floor about the same time as the soles of my bare feet, and picked up speed, spinning across the floor, finally coming to rest against the leg of the stark white chair, which was covered in imported raw silk. It was too white for any ass to sit on, not even mine, and I thought I was a cute bitch. I only bought it to make a statement, to complement the jade walls, the designer comforter set that cost more than two months' salary, the Mosaic vase shipped from St. Martin, and the white doors and trim painted in semigloss, shiny and smooth to the touch. But most importantly, the chair brought out the slightest bit of white in the rather large frameless abstract, hanging just above my bed. Fats used only warm soothing colors as the primary focus: blue, peach, green, chartreuse, some gray and brown. He said when I felt agitated that I should lose myself in it. Embrace the love, security, and peace that it was meant to give. That shit didn't work last night—can't say that I even tried. I did everything I could to block his ass out. I must say, I did enjoy cutting those Armani suits into tiny pieces. I left the tags on. Motherfucker thought he could buy anything, so maybe he could pay somebody to sew that shit back together like new.

Baby First Step stared down at me from the dresser with a look of disappointment on her face. She was still wrapped in plastic inside the box, not a blonde hair out of place, a gift from Daddy one Christmas long ago. Pretty things, I was surrounded by pretty things—not to be touched. I was pretty, or so I was told. I was better at self-destruction than being a trophy bitch; tearing myself apart was so much easier.

I wasn't about to let him get away. I jumped to my feet, threw my yellow nightgown on, and ran toward the bedroom door. My face was tight. I hated my feet getting dirty, but there was no time to stop for shoes.

"Fuck," I screamed out as a sharp pain pierced my foot. Hopping on one leg while holding my foot in the air, I sat on the edge of the bed and pulled a jagged piece of glass from the bottom of my foot. Brown liquor stained the wall in front of me, and I made a mental note to get it repainted. A vague memory of shattering glass, dulled by liquor, masked the pain.

"Damn, I must've been fucked up." I reached over and snatched an empty Heineken bottle from the nightstand, clutching it close to my thigh. I took the steps two at a time, leaving a trail of blood, a steady drip as if I were a hemophiliac, down the stairs, across the foyer, and out the front door.

It was a brisk fall day. My yellow nightgown was flapping in the wind, and my swinging breasts were trying to keep up with the exaggeration of my head movement. My hair stood straight up on top of my head in dire need of combing.

"You black bastard!" I screamed from my front porch. "I picked up your dry cleaning—did your ass a favor—but a bitch can't be nice to you. That spot is in my name. Did you forget I have a key?"

He kept right on stepping. I hated to be ignored. Even in my madness, I was drawn in by that sexy swagger and smooth, dark skin; I undressed every inch of that muscular physique underneath the tan Burberry trench. He walked with confidence in those honey-colored gators, a perfect match to his eyes, and slightly swung the leather briefcase like a man of influence with a sense of purpose.

"Why Chloe? Why did you have to fuck my best friend?" The tears started up again. I hated feeling weak. I was losing control. "Motherfucker, did you hear me?" I screamed in a high-pitched squeal.

Fats stopped in his tracks and turned to face me while removing his signature dark shades. His eyes narrowed as he spoke in a low and threatening tone. "I thought it was you. I was fucked up and trippin' off that boat."

"You lying bastard."

"Amber, you make it real hard to walk away, but I'm a man. I'll never put my hands on you, like that bitch you married. I don't have to explain shit to your ass. Remember, you're not my woman by choice. Now take your half-white ass back in the house. Stop embarrassing yourself. I don't have time for this shit!" He motioned toward the briefcase with a tilt of his head, like I should give a shit that it was filled with kilos of cocaine. "I'll be back for the rest of my stash. That shit got your ass all geeked up."

He spun around, reached into the pocket of his coat, pulled out his keys, and pointed toward the car. The alarm chirped. The doors unlocked. He reached for the handle.

"Embarrassed! I'll show you embarrassed. Try explaining how the fuck your tired ass got clocked upside the head!" I drew back and sent the Heineken bottle flying. It flipped over several times in midair, sailed right past his head, bounced off the roof of the car, and splintered into hundreds of pieces as it crashed against the concrete.

"Your ass is crazy!" Fats yelled.

He jumped into his silver Mercedes coupe and sped off, burning rubber and surely hoping that none of the neighbors heading to church had witnessed the royal cussing out that I delivered as if I were preaching the word on that fine Sunday morning.

A sudden chill jumped my bones like the flu. My yellow cheeks felt flushed. Dark clouds moved in overhead. The wind began to stir. Dead leaves were rustled like cattle by the air. I looked down and realized I was half-naked. Retreating into the house, I closed the door and secured the lock, crossing my arms tightly against my chest for warmth. I shut the vertical blinds and cut off the lights. Uneasiness crept up my spine. It was all too clear as I sat down on the edge of the ottoman, the rain and wind pounding against the windowpane—a thunderstorm was fast approaching. As I rocked back and forth, the salty tears streamed down my face. I'd lived my whole life in denial. I was the mirror image of my mother, and now I feared that I was becoming her.

3

Summer 1963

My mother, a beautiful individual inside and out, was extremely shy, soft spoken, and somewhat of an introvert. Reading was her favorite pastime. She could always be found in the same corner of the kitchen, where the sunlight shone brightly through the window, highlighting the words on each page. Silently, she wished that she could blend into the background—if only the voices would let her—just like the old wooden frame that housed the tarnished picture, which was seldom looked upon.

Daddy always said, "Thunderstorms are God's work. Nothing to be afraid of."

Leaping and twirling across the neatly manicured front lawn of our redbrick row house, I went from ballet to the Watusi, shaking my ass as if I were getting paid. I kicked off my plastic flips-flops, watched them fly through the air and land where they may, and loved the feel of the heavily soaked grass between my toes. With each turn I'd reach back and run my fingers along the nape of my neck, swatting at the irritating price tag still clinging to my brand new red and blue bathing suit. Mommy bought it for me at the Thursday sale, straight off the clearance table at Landsburgh Department store.

The lightning bolts lit the stage as if on cue. The drum roll of thunder clapped loudly in the near distance. The syncopated beat of the rain kissed the leaves, hugged the chiseled bark of the old oak tree, and rhythmically overflowed the drain spout. Metal chimes swinging freely from the chipped and rotted ceiling of the porch two doors down quickened the concerto, accompanied by a sudden gust of wind. There was music all around. All you had to do was listen.

While turning slowly on tiptoes, I saw the tail end of the Emerson's milk truck splash some unsuspecting passerby, who was now wet from head to toe and shouted, "You inconsiderate bastard!" The driver, oblivious to his evil deed, kept right on going. I giggled out loud, covering my mouth with both hands. I glimpsed Mr. Diodorus, whom I affectionately referred to as Mr. D—I never could get his name quite right, the older Greek gentleman who lived next door and whose face was like an aged Frank Sinatra—as he peered through the curtain and stared with a disapproving eye.

Mr. D was my buddy. He'd sit in the shade of the green awning on his newly reconstructed back porch and tell me the most wonderful stories. His son-in-law, a carpenter by trade, worked tirelessly on weekends to finish the job before the summer's heat became unbearable. Daddy was there sweating, sawing, and pounding nails into planks of wood right beside him. Just like always, he was ready to help out anyone in the neighborhood with a need.

Mr. D's pasty white skin was hidden by a starched white long-sleeve shirt, buttoned all the way to the neck, and washed out blue overalls with traces of Clorox. His feet were covered with thick white socks and woven leather sandals that leaned heavily to the right. He wore a faded straw hat with a wide brim, tattered along the edges. He reached up, removed the hat, used it as a fan, and sat it on his lap just long enough to wipe the sweat streaming down his forehead with the back of his hand. He looked hot as hell, sweating like a pig underneath all those clothes and getting hotter by the minute just watching me as I sat on the steps, directly in the sun, soaking up every glorious ray in my lemon yellow seersucker short set, slurping grape Kool-Aid through a straw.

"Those figs look ripe," Mr. D said, pointing toward the tree with a bony index finger extended from a shaky hand with skin so thin it was almost translucent in color, sprinkled with age spots and green veins.

"I'll get you some." I was on my feet and down the steps before he could even ask, reaching up to pluck the sweet-smelling fruit.

Over time the tree had grown over the metal fence into our back-yard, but Daddy didn't complain, cause Mr. D would say with that thick Greek accent, "Take as many as you like."

I used my top like a basket, cradling the figs close to my chest, exposing my belly button, and carefully climbing the steps, no longer able to see my feet. Kicking the screen door with my foot, I yelled out for Mrs. D. "Come to the back door, please. I have figs for your husband."

"No need to scream, child. I'm right here." She stood in the door-way and looked down at me, shaking her head. "To be so little, you have such a big mouth."

"Everybody says that," I responded with a wide grin.

"Then it must be true. I'll take those. Thank you."

"Papa D, you okay?" she asked lovingly of her husband.

He acknowledged with a slight lift of his eyebrow. I bounced down the steps and took a seat, removing the straw from the glass and tak-ing a swallow.

"The sun is no good for you," Mr. D said slowly, with much effort out the good side of his mouth. "Your skin is too fair. You'll burn."

"I love the sun," I replied, tilting my face toward its brightness, placing the glass on the step while I spread my arms to welcome the warmth. "As soon as I'm big enough to climb that ladder," I pointed at the rickety piece of wood leaning against the red brick garage, "you can find me right up there, in just my bathing suit. I want to burn so I can be dark like my daddy."

He shook his head in disagreement. "The sun is no good for you. Your skin is too fair. You'll burn."

He repeated himself a lot. Some days his words were slurred more than others, but I didn't mind. I craved the stories he told about the Greek gods.

"Aphrodite was the goddess of love, beauty, and fertility," said Mr. D.

"She protected the sailors," I chimed in. I left my perch on the steps, walked over to my friend, reached in his left-side pocket, removed the freshly laundered handkerchief his wife placed there each morning, and wiped the drool from the corner of his lip before returning to my place on the steps. He stared off toward the horizon, overcome by a moment of sadness as he realized he'd never quite be the same.

"You're a smart young lady," Mr. D replied as he flashed that half-crooked smile, the sadness gone. "Amber, who is Apollo?"

"I know, I know," I said, waving my hand in the air as if I were in school, competing against the other students for the teacher's attention. I proudly blurted out, "Apollo was the god of music."

"Don't forget prophesy and healing," he said.

"Mr. D, tell me about Medusa again."

"Medusa was a beautiful maiden known for her long, lovely hair. The goddess Athena turned her into a monster."

I moved up a few steps, listening intently.

"Snakes replaced her beautiful locks of hair, and her gaze was so awful it could turn men to stone. Perseus cut her head off on a dare and took it to Athena. She wore it proudly on her breastplate to symbolize the storm clouds."

Goosebumps spread like wildfire over my arms. I knew Medusa and her snakes would crawl into my bed and torment my dreams, but I lingered on his every word.

The sound of tires skidding to the curb shook me from my daydream and forced my attention to the busy avenue. The passenger window of a black sedan slowly rolled down. I recognized him immediately even from a side profile. Dark chocolate skin, long slender fingers with well manicured nails—almost too clean for a man—straight, processed hair combed behind his ear, he looked like he belonged to some singing group. The diamond cluster that was always present on his right pinky finger: no doubt, it was the picture man.

Click. Click.

Two short flashes of light. Our eyes met. Blushing, I remembered the first time he took my picture. Daddy paid him to photograph me at the house.

Perched on top of the brown wooden coffee table with hidden compartments at each end, I wore my crinoline dress with tiny pink rose petals and green stems, white lace anklet socks, and black patent leather shoes with wide buckles. The front and back windows, upstairs and down, were open wide. Not a breeze was stirring in any direction. The picture man took a silk handkerchief from the back pocket of his black slacks, wiped the sweat from his brow, folded the soft material neatly in a small square, and returned it to the same pocket. He went about setting up the camera equipment in spite of the heat.

"Would you care for some fresh lemonade?" Daddy asked the picture man, feeling a bit parched himself.

"Yes, thank you."

Daddy headed toward the kitchen, whistling a carefree tune, light and breezy as if dismissing the heat in his mind. He hadn't turned the corner good before the picture man was right there next to me, so close I could feel his lips brush against my ear as he began to whisper.

"You're so beautiful."

He took my chin in his hand and looked into my light brown eyes a second too long as he helped me pose for the camera, smoothing my dress, his hand resting on my thigh. I felt the warmth in my cheeks turn a rosy pink.

"Perfect. Now smile for the camera."

Mr. D was now standing on his porch, struggling to balance his fragile body on the wooden cane. Usually soft spoken, he pointed his cane and bellowed in my direction, "Go in the house!"

I jumped, spun around, and took off running up the stairs and into the house, leaving my flip-flops on the lawn. The black sedan peeled away from the curb into the steady stream of traffic, in between a Lincoln and a Ford disappearing down the avenue.

4

The dark brocade curtains were drawn tight. All the lights were off except the glow from the television displaying a screen of horizontal lines. I blinked, adjusting my eyes to the dark. Soaking wet, a small puddle formed at my feet.

"Mommy? Mommy, are you there?" Silence.

On my toes I ran my fingers along the wall, fishing for the light switch, the hardwood floor creaking beneath my weight. Flip. The light was comforting.

"Turn off that damn light," Mommy snarled.

I flipped the switch and turned toward the sound of the voice. A flash of lightning sliced through the dining room window, enough for me to catch a glimpse of her kneeling in the corner, her fingers entwined, clasped tightly as if praying. The snake plant, curled and brown on the tips, seemed attached to her head from the ragged wooden table behind her, an altar of half-dead plants thirsting for water. A vision of Medusa came into my head.

"I see you watching! I'm no fool!" Mommy screamed at the television. "I'm too smart to let you lurk between the channels, feeding off my family. You slithering bastard! It won't happen. Not on my watch!" She bolted from the corner and ran toward the television with her fists clenched.

I was used to the mumblings underneath her breath, but for weeks now she had become more outspoken and belligerent.

"Mommy, who are you talking to?" I asked, frightened and backing against the wall.

"The demons in the television." She reached behind the TV and snatched the cord from the electrical socket. Squeezing the chord tightly with both hands, she spoke through gritted teeth. "Shut your ass up now, didn't I?" She flung the cord against the wall and watched it drop to the floor, lifeless and still. Her breathing was labored. I watched her chest rise and fall, praying she wouldn't have an asthma attack. She walked to the sofa where she began rocking back and forth, pulling long strands of hair from her tangled ponytail while staring into the dark screen.

"Come sit next to me," Mommy said.

I did as I was told. We sat perfectly still while the wind howled like a wounded dog, and she continued with her incessant mumbling. The lightning was intense, striking the old oak tree, sending a huge branch crashing to the ground. The street lamps flickered twice, followed by complete darkness. The imminent roar of thunder sounded like a giant bowling ball crashing through the front door for the end-all strike. I jumped in Mommy's arms.

"Girl, what you doing wet?" Mommy questioned, suddenly focusing on me. "Go take that bathing suit off before you catch your death of cold. Put on your pajamas. It's time for you to go to bed."

The voices robbed her of sleep and gnawed at her exceptional beauty like a dog on a bone. Her face was drawn and pasty. Dark circles outlined her light gray eyes. The sparkle was gone, replaced by a dead stare that bore a hole through anything in its path.

She'd been up for an entire week, pacing the floor, up and down the staircase, opening and slamming doors. Her voice was hoarse, but she continued to ramble. Her tongue darted in and out repeatedly, licking at dried blood that formed in the corner of her parched lips. Then silence.

I closed my eyes, wishing for sleep and counting the drops of rainwater hitting the bottom of the metal bucket. Daddy said he'd fix that leak weeks ago. I felt myself drifting off; maybe now I could get some sleep.

My eyes sprang open. I heard her taking the steps two at a time. I was wide awake when she burst through my bedroom door. Eyes bloodshot and glazed, she held onto a mound of hair she'd ripped from the root, her ponytail an unruly mess. Spit flew as she stood over my bed swinging wildly.

"I told you to stay the fuck away from my child! I'll kill all you sons of bitches in here!"

I grabbed the pillow and placed it in front of me like a shield. Pressing my small frame against the headboard, clutching the pillow, I was afraid of my own mother.

"Mommy, please don't!" I screamed.

She took a deep breath and let out a long sigh of relief. Her arms slowly settled at her thighs. "You can go back to sleep now, baby. I'll never let anyone hurt you." She pivoted and left the room.

I followed her down the stairs. She lay crumpled and spent on the sofa, rapidly blinking, trying to focus on a page of the encyclopedia but straining without her glasses. Mozart played in the background. Her IQ was through the roof! Her mind was never at rest. It soaked up information like a sponge, though she was constantly fighting a battle to hold on to her sanity.

I tiptoed to the front door, turned the lock slowly, and pulled hard. I struggled with the screen door, the wind and rain trying to hold me prisoner.

"Where do you think you're going?"

Mommy was on my ass. I laid my weight into the door and took off down the front steps. The rain broke my stride and beat me down. My pajamas were soaked, the material clinging to my body like a second layer of skin. Slipping as I hit the bottom concrete step, my hands flailed in the air, reaching out in desperation. I briefly grabbed hold of the wet handrail, saving my ass long enough to break my fall. I cut across Mr. D's flower bed, and I saw a spiderweb—swollen like a blood-soaked wad of cotton, glistening with fresh raindrops, and stretched atop a low-lying crepe myrtle—bite the dust as I trampled it beneath my speeding feet. Drenched to the bone, tears washed away by rainwater, I was scared as shit with Mommy right behind me. The high beams from a dark sedan parked on the corner flashed on and off. Instinctively, I covered my eyes, shielding them from the blinding light. I felt Mommy's hand on my back, faked to the left and spun out wide, dodging her grip—too many nights of playing tag under the stars. I was too fast to be easily caught. She slipped on the mud and went down. I looked back but kept booking, quickening my pace, relieved to see Ms. Lola's front door opening.

"Good morning, heartache, you old friend of mine. Good morning, heartache, thought I said good-bye last night," Ms. Lola sang. She was seated behind the baby grand, painfully belting out the lyrics of the Billie Holiday classic. The piano was her latest toy, a gift to herself. She even gave it a name, "Baldwin." Funny kind of name for a piano, but she sure must've liked it 'cause she had it printed in white lettering right across the front so everyone could see.

Swaying from side to side, lost in the words to the song, eyes shut tight, Ms. Lola lit into the chords, caressing those black-and-white ivory keys with the intensity of a seasoned jazz singer. She ignored the raunchy conversation taking place just across the room while Stevie Wonder, the thirteen-year-old blind boy some referred to as a musical genius, filtered through the speakers.

"Man, you gonna play your hand or get a motherfucking room?" said the skinny man with the wide gap, receding hairline, and bulging pockets to the older guy with mixed gray hair sitting directly across the table. The older man had his eyes fixed on the woman with the see-through dress and no underwear, while scratching his ass.

I knew Ms. Lola was two sheets to the wind when she reached up with her thumb and index finger and flipped her neatly cut bangs, damp with perspiration, to expose a seldom-seen, slightly large forehead that shone brightly in stark competition with the pear-shaped diamonds sitting square in the middle of her earlobes, which slightly sagged from the weight. Her carrot-red hair—usually swept up tight in a chignon, freshly permed and colored—was resting on her shoulders, the humidity giving it a soft fluffy look like cotton candy. She was strikingly beautiful, minus the heavily painted ruby-red lips, dark mascara, and powdered foundation she applied each day for her public.

She sang from her heart, as if every word were a memory best left in the past. She actually had a pretty good singing voice, although her skills on the piano were a little rusty. Hitting a wrong key, she paused, opened her eyes, and fumbled as if she was in complete darkness. She searched for the burning cigarette in the ashtray on top of the piano, took a long drag, curling her lips to the side and exhaling the smoke, and then she placed the cigarette perfectly on the edge of the ashtray without looking, a practiced habit. Now staring at the piano keys, shifting her fingers a little to the right, she began again from the top. Yeah, she was twisted all right. That was the only time she sang that song.

I slipped right past some old drunk who was saying his good-nights, staggering from one side of the doorway to the other with his penis in his hand, and peeing into the wind. I jetted through the front door, right past the men who were sipping on bourbon and smoking stinky cigars around the rectangular-shaped dining table to my left while women in short, tight dresses with painted faces and false eyelashes rubbed their backs in a circular motion, leaning in close to whisper seductively in their ears and briefly interrupt the concentration on their hands. They were all too busy to notice my entrance.

There was a whole lot going on at Ms. Lola's: numbers, bootleg liquor, nightly poker games, and just about anything else you desired. If she didn't have it, she knew where to get it for a price. She was on a dollar hard. Daddy didn't mind that I spent so much time there. He said Ms. Lola had a good heart.

"Help me!" I screamed loudly, sprinting as if the devil himself was on my ass, desperately seeking a safe haven, and running straight toward Ms. L, like an arrow to a bull's-eye. I tripped over my own feet, and the floor raced toward my face.

She sprang to her feet, pushing the piano bench backward with the calves of a long-distance runner. Her last-minute catch was that of a benched quarterback with a get-out-of-jail-free pass making the winning play of the game. She cradled my tiny body close to her own as if she had birthed me. I held on tight and buried my face in the side of her neck, embraced by the soft scent of her signature fragrance, Chanel No. Five. A wet stain kissed the front of her skirt set.

"What's wrong, child? You look like you've seen a fucking ghost!"

I remained tearful but silent, fearing the worst was yet to come. The smell of fish frying on the kitchen stove made me remember I'd gone to bed hungry. I eyed the spread on the dining room table: fish and chicken dipped in flour, milk, and secret seasonings, fried to a deep golden brown just like I liked it, plus ribs so tender they were falling off the bone, and yellow potato salad. Some people made potato salad with mayo and no mustard, but I didn't eat that shit, no way. My eyes skipped to the collard greens mixed with kale. My stomach began to growl.

Elena, the housekeeper, charged out of the kitchen. Her long coal-black hair, parted down the middle, masked her face like a veil. Her hands were covered in flour, her red-and-white-checkered apron was flying, and she swung a cast-iron frying pan in midair, ready to go to battle for her employer.

"Lola, give me my child." All eyes turned toward the front door. Mommy was bent over in the doorway, hands resting on both knees, mouth agape, gasping for air, her chest rising and falling at an uneven pace.

I jumped from Ms. Lola's arms, hitting the hardwood floor with a thud and hid behind her big ass, the same one I'd watched so many men follow around the room with lust in their eyes, never saying a word. Mommy's presence in the doorway was followed by an eerie wind that sailed up under the playing cards, lifting them above the table and dropping them back down again—a wind that sent my teeth to chattering.

Ms. Lola searched for those beautiful eyes, which turned from gray to green depending on Mommy's temperament or the change of seasons, now dull and covered with a cloudy film; the shine was gone, swallowed up by a macerated face.

"Baby, let me get you some water," Ms. Lola said in a voice filled with compassion. She walked to the dining room table with me clinging to her skirt tail, picked up the water pitcher, dripping with condensation, and poured the cold liquid into a tall glass.

Mommy was covered in mud. The quick-paced rise and fall of Mommy's chest returned to normal. She stood wide legged in a defensive stance. "Do I look like I need water, bitch? Give me my child!"

As Mommy spoke, a lightning bolt lit the sky and revealed dark brown nipples standing at attention on a pair of tits big enough to swallow a small child whole. Her eyes danced from face to face, took an individual snapshot of the card players and whores that surrounded them, and finally rested upon Ms. Lola, looking her up and down as if sizing up the enemy. Smoke from lit cigars smoldering in metal ashtrays swirled around the staring faces, traveled toward the ceiling, and escaped out the open front door.

Elena lifted the needle from the vinyl record. The music stopped along with the mouths of the shit-talking men gathered around the card table, who sat their drinks down, not knowing what to expect next. The cuckoo clock, mounted in the far corner of the dining room, overlooking the massive wooden table that set eight, sounded once. The entire room shifted their gaze to the yellow canary, breaking an uneasy silence momentarily.

"Dee, the child is going to stay here tonight. She's safe here."

"She belongs with me!" Mommy screamed, running toward the table, smashing an empty glass against the wood, and grasping the jagged edges by the base as she held it out in a threatening gesture toward Ms. Lola. That crazed look returned to her eyes. There was something very dark in her gestures.

"Dee, have I ever lied to you?" Ms. Lola said in a very calm, soothing voice. "No one will hurt her. You have my word. Now put the glass down."

Mommy turned her head to the left as if someone had called out her name. Her attention focused on the fat bald man with piercing eyes, who was sucking on his teeth and obviously upset about the interruption of the card game. She lit right into him.

"I know you want to fuck me, you fat bastard. I got a husband that takes real good care of me. I ain't never wanted for dick. You'll never even get close enough to smell this pussy." She spat the words like venom as she flung the glass toward his face.

He ducked. Furious, he raised his left hand and stroked the back of his neck, contemplating his next move. He abruptly stood up, popping several buttons on his snug-fitting polyester shirt, sending them sailing like tiny spinning tops, one landing in the corner next to a potted plant, the other bouncing off Ms. L's drink with a clink before hitting the hardwood floor. His hairy stomach was exposed.

"Now that bitch has gone too far."

Ms. Lola lifted her skirt and pulled the pistol from her garter pointing it at the fat man.

"Don't move, motherfucker." The fat man froze where he stood. "Sit your ass down."

He flushed and glanced around the room, attempting to read the reaction of the other men. Breathing hard through flared nostrils, he took a seat.

Ms. Lola looked down at me and said, "Go on upstairs, dry off, and get a pair of pajamas out my dresser drawer. You can sleep in my bed. Go on now."

I hurried up the stairs, stopping midway. Desi, Elena's badass son, was sitting at the top of the stairs, watching all the action. He raised his finger to his lips, signaling me to keep quiet. Continuing up the staircase to the top, I took a seat right beside him.

"Elena, you keep an eye on these fuckers," Ms. Lola said, handing over the pistol to her Spanish housekeeper. "If anyone raises an eyebrow wrong, shoot 'em."

"Yes, Ms. Lola," Elena said with authority, placing the pistol in her waistband and her hands on her imaginary hips. "All right, gentlemen, let's get back to the game," Elena said, placing the needle back on the 33, turning the stereo up, and singing loudly to Stevie Wonder's "Fingertips." "Everybody say yeah." she clapped her hands to the beat, and a small dusting of flour fell to the floor.

"Elena, I know I said I was taking a break from smoking that shit, but have a fat one rolled and waiting for me when I get back. I think I might need it," Ms. Lola said, her voice trailing off to a whisper. Elena smiled.

Walking toward the closet, Ms. Lola turned the knob and opened the door. Mommy stood guard at the front door, staring out into the rain, and speaking to no one in particular—incoherent mumblings in a rushed tone.

"Surely you must've seen the snakes crawling out the gutter." She said. "There were thousands of them. How could you have missed their presence, squeezing through the cracks, up the pipes, slithering into my home, laying in wait? They were trying to take my child."

"I'll take care of the snakes. Don't you worry."

Ms. Lola stood very still, smoothing the edges of her carrot-red hair, gathering her thoughts, and wondering what was yet to come. She pushed the beige camel hair and the black lambswool swing coats to the side and slipped the black raincoat off the wooden hanger. As she turned her head away from the garments, the lit Camel cigarette dangling from the edge of her lips, she reached toward the back of the closet and rested her hand on the black umbrella with the silver handle shaped like a naked lady.

She took a long drag off the cigarette, inhaling deeply, squinting from the smoke. She held the glowing tip between two fingers not far in front of her, took one last pull, and crushed the butt in the lead crystal ashtray. She spoke to Elena while walking toward Mommy.

"I'm going down the street to sit with Dee for a while, at least until her husband comes home from work. Damn, I forgot I'm supposed to take Fats school shopping in the morning. Elena, do you mind?"

"Not at all, senorita."

Heading toward the door, Ms. Lola passed by a working girl bent over a mark; drooling out the corner of her mouth, she was high on some real different shit with her ass in the air and puppies damn near falling out of a dress two sizes too small. Ms. Lola began to wrinkle her nose as she caught a whiff of rank pussy. She looked truly offended. She turned and approached the woman. "Sweetie."

"You talking to me?" the unkempt whore asked, her speech slow and slurred, knees bent. She reached down and scratched her thigh with light pink nails, badly in need of a manicure.

"No, I'm talking to your motherfucking twin in the corner. Step over here for a minute." Ms. Lola motioned with a wave of her fingers. The room fell silent once again. The regulars knew that tone.

The whore took short, unsure steps.

"You're trying to get some cash. I can relate." Ms. Lola paused, the stern lines just above her brow softened, as if she felt some empathy for the woman. What little compassion felt was gone as Ms. Lola stared the whore down. "Don't ever come into my home trying to turn a trick with a dripping snatch and a foul odor." Her voice got a little higher. "Half these Negroes got wives. I can't send them home with burnt dicks. Rule of the house: only disease-free pussy is allowed on the premises. You need to get the fuck out." Her tone was threatening.

"Damn, Ms. Lola, you don't have to be so cold," the whore said, clutching her purse close, nervously pulling at the hem of her dress. She hurried toward the front door, eyes to the floor, avoiding the unwanted stares bearing down on her.

"Now what was I saying?" Ms. Lola stroked the corner of her eyebrow, a look of bewilderment on her face.

Elena chimed in from the kitchen, "You asked me to take Fats shopping in the morning."

"Damn. That's right."

"Desi can sleep in late. He and Amber can play until you get back."

Upon hearing Ms. L's comments, I folded my arms tight across my flat chest, feeling my rib cage just below, and dropped my bottom lip, perturbed, thinking I didn't want to play with Desi. That boy stayed in trouble. Just last week, he set Mr. Jacobs's garage on fire while Fats stood guard below. I watched Desi's sneaky ass scale the side of Mr. Jacobs's boat, slip through an unlocked window, and minutes later crawl right back out through that same window, jump to the ground and take off running with Fats in pursuit as the garage erupted in flames.

Mr. Jacobs owned the barbershop next to the greasy spoon carryout with the good fries. He was a regular customer at Ms. Lola's, putting that hard-earned money right back into the community. Ms. Lola was pissed.

"I promise you. This is hurting me more than it's hurting you," Elena said as she beat the shit out of Desi's curly headed ass. Fats got beat, too, for lying.

"Momma, I swear we were in Rock Creek Park hunting for frogs. Don't hit me no more, please," Fats begged, twisting from side to side, reaching behind him, and wrapping his hand tightly around the source of punishment, hoping to avoid the sting of the black leather belt his mother swung so freely.

"Oh, so you want to grab the belt. Wrong move, little boy. Strip down to your drawers."

Fats fell silent as he disrobed. His tee shirt and shorts lay crumpled on the floor. He showed no fear as he raised his eyes to meet his mother's cold glare. This time Ms. Lola swung the belt even harder, leaving visible red whelps on his dark skin. She hated a liar.

"Cole puts a hurting on flapjacks and bacon. He can feed the kids," Ms. Lola said as an afterthought.

"You know the picture man loves to gamble," Elena said almost singing the words, her Spanish accent thick. "No telling when he'll get home."

"He knows better than to cross my doorsill with the sun trailing his ass like a lovesick mistress." Pausing, she stood completely still as if pondering her last words. Ms. Lola looked past Mommy out the open front door and felt the rain cross the doorsill as she walked toward her. She spoke again, this time losing the attitude.

"Then again," Ms. Lola continued, "who am I fooling? That man got gypsy in his blood. He might just up and leave one day with not so much as a good-bye."

"Better play it safe. If I'm not back before you're ready to leave, take the kids to Ms. Annie's. She owes me for some numbers," Ms. Lola said.

"She'll be glad to babysit. Work off that bill."

Draping the raincoat over Mommy's shoulders, Ms. Lola opened the umbrella wide enough for two, took Mommy's hand into her own, squeezed it gently, and led her best friend out the door, hoping to save her from herself.

Mommy fought hard but slowly slipped away.

5

The heat of the sun, bearing down on the left side of my face through an opening in the flowered drapes, forced one eye open and woke me from a peaceful slumber, the first I'd remembered in months. Sprawled out on my stomach, I took total advantage of the king-size bed. Rolling onto my back, I swung a bare leg to the right side of the bed and stretched my toes wide like mini antennae in search of Ms. Lola's body heat, a sense of warmth and protection. I recoiled from the cold sheets still tucked tightly beneath the mattress and the undisturbed bedspread, and jerked all five toes back to the warm side. I sat up, realizing that she must still be with Mommy. I frantically rubbed my itching nose, allergic to the white lilies and baby's breath so beautifully arranged in a crystal vase on top of the mahogany dresser.

White lilies, the same pattern as the bedspread and the curtains, were Ms. L's favorite. Yesterday's rain had cooled things off just long enough to bring on another scorcher. Most of August had been dry, every day ninety-eight degrees or better.

My pajama top was bunched around my neck, exposing my belly button and beebee knots, as Mommy affectionately called them. The bottoms were discarded sometime during the night, lost in the covers. Daddy always said I was a wild sleeper. He awoke many a night with my feet in his face. Blindly feeling for my bottoms, I grasped the cotton material and slipped one leg on after the other. The elastic waistband was a little loose, and I pulled the bottoms high up over my stomach.

The familiar smell of frying bacon, scrambled eggs, and warm buttered toast was absent from the air. The house was quieter than ever. My stomach began to growl. I held it in tightly, trying to make the annoying rumble go away.

Sitting on the side of the bed, I slipped off the double mattress, feeling my feet disappear into the depth of the plush white carpet. I scurried down the hallway to Fats and Desi's bedroom. Both beds were unmade and empty. Stepping out into the hallway, I turned my attention to the west wing. The newly built addition was off limits to us kids, just like the locked room in the far end of the basement. Curious, I looked around to make sure I was alone and ventured down the hallway toward forbidden territory, carefully avoiding the wooden floorboards that squeaked.

The door was ajar to the first bedroom. I peered inside. The windows were bare. A ladder lay flush against the wall next to the window. Large cans of paint, wooden brushes in various sizes, and a tin pan sat in the middle of the floor on top of old crumpled sheets. Muffled voices could be heard from the adjoining bedroom. I'd already seen a man's penis a little earlier; maybe if I stayed really quiet, I might see that and some ass. Dropping to my knees, I crawled up to the bedroom door and got up close to the keyhole. The metal felt cold against my eyelid. Desi was on his knees; the picture man sat on the edge of the bed, his penis inside Desi's mouth.

"Stop crying, little man," the picture man said as he held the boy's head with both hands slowly guiding his penis in and out. "You'll learn to like it," he said, while closing his eyes, tilting his head way back, his mouth slightly ajar, lost in the pleasure of the young boy's mouth.

My heart began to race, beating so loudly I thought my chest would burst. I was frozen to the spot with fear, my eye glued to the keyhole. My mind said run, but my legs were numb; I began to crawl along the baseboard like a cockroach, staying below the radar. Halfway down the hallway, I found my legs, jumped to my feet, and tipped into the boys' bedroom, where I hid in the closet underneath a pile of mud-stained shirts, funky sweat socks, and underwear with skid marks. I shook like a leaf on a tree, fighting back the urge to cry out for help. Clasping my hands together, I silently prayed.

A sound filtered underneath the closet door like the whimpering of a newborn pup. Slowly pushing the door open, I peered out. Desi was rocking back and forth, repeatedly opening and closing a cigarette lighter, staring at the flame. Leaving my safe place, compelled to go to him, I walked to the edge of the bed, reached out, and placed my hand on his shoulder.

"It's okay, Desi," I said while stroking his back. "I saw the picture man. I saw him hurt you. You've got to tell."

He pounced quickly, leaping from the bed to his feet, knocking me off balance with the weight of his body. He wrapped both hands around my neck, squeezing, pinning my back against the wall. Face to face, I could feel his hot breath as he spoke with contempt in his eyes. "Bitch, if you tell anyone...I'll kill you." He squeezed tighter. "Understand me?"

Gasping for air, face flushed, eyes bulging, I nodded my head in deference. He finally released his grip. Sliding down the wall, I crouched in a squatting position and rubbed my neck, dabbing at the tears that escaped from the corners of my eyes. I stared at Desi in disbelief. He walked back to the bed, sat down, and stared right back at me, as if he was looking straight through me. It took a few minutes for me to catch my breath. I was confused, replaying the events of the morning in my head, but I knew I had to get out of there. I ran out the bedroom past Desi and crept down the stairs. Pancakes dripping with warm butter and maple syrup and bacon sizzling in hot grease engulfed my nostrils and set my stomach to stirring. My heart beat even faster as I neared the landing.

"Are the stars out tonight? I don't know if it's sunny or bright. I only have eyes for you," the picture man sang. It was one of my favorite songs by the Flamingos. My brother Chris played it so much I knew every word. I'd stand on his feet, and he would waltz me around the room to that same tune.

Ms. Lola lay passed out on the sofa, flat on her back, mouth wide open, snoring like a man. A half-empty bottle of vodka, a watered-down drink, and an ashtray full of burnt cigarette butts sat on the coffee table within reach. I turned toward her, willing her eyes to open, hoping she would feel my need. I wondered if I should wake her from her drunken slumber and tell her that her lover was a child molester. The same man who made her howl late at night, like a wounded dog, got his nut off with little kids. My mind said run.

I slipped out the front door barefoot, and hit the cement steps full speed. "Ouch. Ouch." On the hot sidewalk, I shifted from one foot to the other as if playing hopscotch. The heat tortured the soles of my feet, sealing my pact with the Devil, where I agreed to hold my tongue, keeping a dark, dirty secret between two friends, who were now enemies.

6

"Stay the fuck away from me!" Mommy screamed, swinging wildly at the two hospital attendants as the butcher knife sliced through the air.

"Mommy, please stop!" I screamed through the tears. "I don't want them to hurt you."

From the top of the steps, I stood by helpless. Chris did his best to console me while fighting back the tears himself. The entire block was watching as the men in white coats escorted my mother from our home, bound in a straightjacket. I was young but not naïve. This time she would be gone far longer than the times before. She fought every step of the way, cursing, spitting, and kicking, barely recognizing us as she was whisked out the front door.

"Hayden, let me take her. It won't be a problem," Ms. Lola said with genuine concern.

With tears in his eyes my father responded, "Thank you, Lola, for offering, but it's important to me that my family stays together."

"Come on, kid. Let's go for a ride," Chris said while blinking the tears away. He grabbed my hand and pulled me through the crowd of onlookers toward the car. He released my hand, which I allowed to fall numbly to my side, while he felt his left pants pocket for his keys, now ten steps ahead of me.

Let's go for a ride. I thought to myself, "Ride number one hundred thirty-seven and counting." Which one was this, the one to make me feel better? Or maybe it's the one to make me forget the hurt and embarrassment I'd just endured in front of the entire block. Maybe this was the ride of all rides to make it all disappear. My face felt flushed, not from the sun but from pent up anger.

Suddenly my world stood still. I stopped dead in my tracks. "I don't want to go for a fucking ride," I mumbled under my breath.

Chris looked back, realizing I had stopped walking. He motioned with his hand. "Come on, kid."

"I don't want to go for a fucking ride!" I screamed. "Not with you, not with Daddy. You all can go straight to hell!"

The dam broke. I began to run straight into oncoming traffic, screaming, "I want my mommy back." I don't remember Chris snatching me from harm's way. I had stopped struggling by the time we reached the car, and he buckled me in with the seat belt.

I stared out the window in silence. The first several blocks down Georgia Avenue were filled with red brick storefronts on every corner, boarded up apartment buildings used by junkies as shooting galleries, beauty parlors, barbershops, and liquor stores consumed by one continuous never-ending tear. Chris was driving like a reckless teenager stoned out of his mind, pushing the limit.

"Cheer up," Chris said while patting the top of my head. "I'm going to see if I can get us in the show."

He led me down an alley just off Seventh and T Street to the back entrance of the famous Howard Theater. Knock, knock. Chris stepped back as a burly giant of a man opened the door. "I'm here to see Margie."

Margie was a member of a singing group called the Jewels, who were getting a lot of recognition as an opening act for famous headliners on the chitlin circuit, such as James Brown, the Temptations, Patti LaBelle and the Bluebells, Smoky Robinson and the Miracles, the Supremes, and many more. She and Chris were friends from school.

Their dressing room, not much larger than a closet, was just beyond the back door entrance.

"Hey, Margie. I brought my little sister for the show."

"She's a cutie! What's your name?" Margie inquired while giving her freshly painted face a once over in the mirror.

"Amber," I replied just above a whisper. I was in awe of the pretty ladies in sequined gowns and high-heeled shoes.

"You two go on out front and take a seat before the paying customers start to arrive."

We took our seats on the first row, center orchestra. I was so close I could see the scuffmarks on the hardwood floor of the stage; some were surely left from James Brown's fancy footwork.

The stage lights began to dim as the theater came alive with the buzz of hushed voices and the shuffle of feet as patrons hurried to take a seat. The house band cranked up. The emcee appeared on stage in a shiny suit and introduced the Jewels in a deep baritone voice. The spotlights changed color, setting the mood for each song. The sequined gowns transformed in front of my eyes. The audience began to dance in the aisles, singing and clapping along with the ladies on the stage as if everyone was a part of the act. My eyes grew large as saucers as I tried to drink in every movement.

Several acts followed before the headliners were introduced. You could feel the intensity of the crowd grow as the emcee stepped on stage.

"It is indeed an honor for the Howard Theater to present to you all the way from Detroit, the Motor City, Smokey Robinson and the Miracles!"

The audience was on their feet, and the applause was deafening. Women rushed to the edge of the stage to get a closer look at the gorgeous man with green eyes and a falsetto voice. Smokey broke into "Ooh Baby Baby" as the women were ushered back to their seats. I stood in my chair struggling to catch a glimpse.

A quiet spread through the theater as every eye and ear sat glued to the hypnotic crooner. An occasional scream from a devoted fan made heads turn, but just for a second.

The Miracles closed the show with "Mickey's Monkey," bringing the entire house to their feet again. Smokey wiped his brow with a white cotton towel and then threw it out into the audience. Two well-dressed women feverously tugged and pulled at the material. He then unbuckled his leather belt and hurled it into space. Chris was on his feet with outstretched arms. His body collided with several others all around me. That's when the fight broke out. I ducked beneath the chair. Above me was the sound of fists against bone. The burley giant and three other bouncers separated the brawlers.

Chris pulled me from beneath the seat into his arms with a broad grin and soon-to-be black eye, clutching Smokey's belt.

The Howard Theater provided me with an escape from the heavy feelings of despair and the deep, dark secrets far more than any child should have to bear and took my love affair with music from vinyl to the stage.

7

I was confined to my bedroom with a case of the mumps—that shit wasn't no joke. It jumped from one side of my face to the other, impregnating each jaw.

The solitude gave me time to hone my skills in the game of jacks. Tweetie, Fats's cousin from down south, was staying at Ms. Lola's for a couple of weeks. She was five years older than me, a cute chocolate drop full of personality but sly as all get-out. Every summer she'd crush me playing jacks. I was ready for her this time.

Jumping to my feet, I stole a quick glance in the oval-shaped mirror that rested securely atop the dresser and was elated with the reflection staring back at me. I placed both hands on my face, patting and caressing the normalcy I'd taken for granted.

Jetting down the stairs, I peeped through the curtained front door, taking in any and all movements outside.

I was overjoyed to see Daddy slowly climbing the front steps, coming home for a short break, exhausted. He worked more hours in a day than the law allowed, chauffeuring important people around in a shiny black limousine.

"Damn, my daddy sure is sharp," I said out loud, 'cause he was looking quite dapper in his Brooks Brothers charcoal-gray suit and burgundy and gray silk tie. I would've given the world for his smooth dark skin, thick wavy hair, and dark brooding eyes that seemed sad even when he smiled. I could've sworn he was half man, half ape as he loosened his tie, leaning his head slightly to the left. When he unbuttoned his white shirt, the chest hairs peeked out the opening.

I loved him so much that I proclaimed to the world that I looked just like him, when in fact I had Mommy's light, bright, damn-near white complexion, thanks to her granddaddy who was straight Caucasian. I never had the pleasure of meeting the man. Shit, who was I fooling? I'm sure he wouldn't have owned up to me anyway, no matter how light I was, with everything being such a deep, dark secret in those days. He was just a sperm donor that marked me for life. I probably could've done the pass-over thing like some of my cousins— they went on up to Boston, some parts of Connecticut, I've heard, and started over as lily white. I got the whole package: long straight hair, a face full of freckles, and light brown eyes with long thick lashes that tickled my face every time I blinked. My small pointed nose turned up on the end and looked like it was hard for me to breathe. My mouth was so tiny and perfect it shocked the shit out of folks who heard me cuss like a sailor. I got it honest, straight from my mommy.

The sofa with the large floral pattern, stained and worn with an annoying broken spring, was a welcome sight to Daddy. Before he lay down, he walked toward the stereo and shifted through the stack of albums underneath. He carefully removed the record from the album jacket, holding it by the edges with the palms of his large dark hands. He lifted the diamond needle, held in place with worn rubber bands and a shiny copper penny, and carefully placed it on the wax. He removed his suit jacket, draped it across the chair, and ran his hand over the material trying to smooth out the wrinkles. He lay down, ignoring the spring nestled in the curve of his back. The sounds of Wes Montgomery filled the room.

"Amber, always cherish the music," Daddy said with his eyelids closed tight. "It's your history. As time goes on and you're a little older, it'll get you through the darkest hours."

"Okay, Daddy. I'll remember," I said, distracted by a fat-ass roach crawling up the leg of the antique mahogany coffee table. Everything in that damn house was old, dark, and heavy. It was like living in a museum. I guess we were rich, if I let Daddy tell it. He'd always say, "Amber, this furniture is worth a lot of money."

Just like the time he and Mommy showed up outside of my elementary school in his favorite hobby, a dilapidated 1947 black Chevy. The seats were worn, and giant rust spots clung to the fading paint job like a flesh-eating disease, providing a clear view straight to the other side of the street.

It was embarrassing. I took off running, grabbed the car door handle, and pulled the heavy door closed behind me as I cradled my body on the floor before anyone could see me.

"Amber, get up off that floor," Daddy said, shaking his head. "This car is going to be worth a lot of money. You just wait until I fix this baby up. Get that engine to purring. The phone will be ringing non-stop with people wanting to buy it for a pretty penny. You'll see."

I made a promise to myself right then and there that when I was all grown up, there would be no antique furniture in my house, and I'd keep a shiny new car parked at the curb. Fuck the pretty penny! But for now, the roach had to go!

Sliding backward on my butt, I slowly reached for the National Geographic magazine beneath the end table; it left a perfect framing of undisturbed dust to mark its spot. I was tempted to write my name but a more important matter was at hand, and I couldn't take my eye off the filthy little insect about to give birth.

"Bam," I squealed, smashing the roach flat. "Got your ass! No offspring this time around. Maybe in another life."

I ran to the kitchen and buried the magazine deep in the trash. It was the last of a stack that sat untouched for years. Mommy said, "Your father is a pack rat. So we'll slowly take these one at a time to the trash and bury them deep. It's the only way that I can clear out this clutter."

I returned to the living room and took a seat on the floor beside Daddy. Tapping my bare foot to the jazz, I watched his belly rise up and down as he snored. I smoothed the hair on his arms, tickled his nose hairs, ran my fingers over those high cheekbones, and watched him make funny faces in his sleep.

There was always music in our house. Mommy used to play Frank Sinatra, Sammy Davis Jr., and Perry Como records while lying underneath the dining room table for hours on end. I'd sometimes crawl under there with her, snuggle up close, and lay my head against those huge breasts, so close I could feel her heart beat.

"Mommy, why do you lay underneath the table?" I'd ask, pulling at a string on her sweater.

Her only reply as she sang along with the records was, "It's peaceful under here." I missed that.

Thirty minutes or so had gone by when Daddy sat straight up, swung his long legs to the floor, and rubbed his bloodshot eyes. He bent down and kissed me on the forehead while rolling down his sleeves, slipped on his suit jacket, leaned toward the bronze oval mirror that hung on the wall just above the sofa, and straightened his tie.

"Gotta go, Amber. Be good," he said as he rushed out the front door.

"Bye, Daddy."

As soon as he pulled off, I ran over and threw the pillows from the couch to the floor, collecting all the silver coins that slipped from his pockets while he slept. For me, it was like hitting the jackpot.

I ran as fast as my little feet could carry me to the basement door and yanked it open. I yelled down the stairs to my brother, "Chris, take me to the store please?"

Chris hollered back, "What did you say? I can't hear you, kid."

The Temptations were harmonizing like shit, Eddie Kendricks in the lead, his falsetto voice pouring out the one good speaker that was still intact on the portable radio. The other one was shot to hell along with a crippled antenna from countless falls from the windowsill. We all took turns, at one point or another, tripping over the cord, watching what was left of a birthday present from Mommy to Chris tumble and fall. You couldn't pay that Negro to throw it away.

"Come on down," he said, still counting his reps.

I knew not to invade his space without an invitation, because I tried that once and got the holy shit slapped out of me.

Every day after football practice, Chris would sneak some hot-ass girl in the back door without Mommy knowing. Fucking like rabbits right underneath her.

I crept down the basement steps once and saw it all for myself. I couldn't see her face; this one was different, dark like Hershey chocolate. Chris usually went for those high yellow hoes from affluent families on upper Sixteenth Street, which was often referred to as the "Gold Coast." He'd charm the shit out of their mothers and talk politics with their dads. The rest was easy. Her thick muscled legs were spread eagle. She was still wearing her sweat socks and black-and-whites—a cheerleader no doubt—and the bottom of her feet were reaching for the ceiling. The pussy made a strange clapping sound as if it was applauding the act. Chris was sweating like a bull with his shorts down around his ankles. I watched his naked ass pumping like shit, his dick so far up in her that she seemed disoriented. I was waiting for that bitch to start speaking in tongues like the ladies in the storefront church on the avenue.

"Stop. No. Please don't." She moaned while meeting his every thrust, clawing at the middle of his back, pulling him in closer. I couldn't help wondering why she was telling him to stop yet holding him so tightly.

Her head thrashed from side to side. I glimpsed her face, twisted and deformed as she bit down hard on her bottom lip. "Oh God!" she screamed and bucked wildly.

I turned and hauled ass up the steps. I hardly slept that night, couldn't wait to see the next day's performance. I slowly opened the basement door and crept down the steps, just like before. I'd barely reached the third step when Chris rose up out of the darkness. I felt my face sting as his hand connected hard against my cheek, blood rushing into the handprint he left on my face.

"Don't come down these steps again without asking." His tone was menacing. Chris was the first man whom I truly loved to hit me. I was hurt and confused. My own daddy didn't hit me. I never said a word to my parents. Neither did Chris. I also never forgot.

Gingerly, I descended the stairs, plopped down on the fifth step, rested my elbows on bony thighs, cradled my face in my hands, and watched his sweaty ass lift weights. His daily ritual was paying off. His body was rock hard.

I understood why the girls followed him home. He was cute as far as brothers go—okay, for real, he was fine as shit. The perfect mix of both parents: dark copper skin, Mommy's eyes, upturned nose and thin top lip; he was hairy like Daddy with a full bottom lip and dark wavy hair. He wore a stocking cap all the time, as if he needed to. I thought for the longest he had a case of ringworm and just hadn't shaved his head like some of the kids at school.

Chris was a straight-A student. It was rumored he fucked his English teacher, Ms. Bannister, a petite woman in her late twenties with horn-rimmed glasses, a tight French roll, and a loose pussy. Women loved him, both young and old.

"Where'd you get money?" Chris said between breaths, still counting.

"Daddy gave it to me." Well, he did in a way; I wasn't really telling a story, I thought to myself, smiling inwardly.

"It stinks down here," I said squeezing my nostrils shut.

Chris sat upright on the mat and put the weights down hard on the cement floor.

"What did Mommy tell you?" Chris said looking directly at me, waiting for an answer.

Avoiding his stare, I bowed my head, chin to chest, in total submission, like a puppy waiting for an ass whipping with the morning newspaper after wetting the floor.

Nervously wringing my hands, I said, "If you don't have something good to say, then say nothing at all. I'm sorry."

I waited a minute before lifting my head. I wanted to appear humble and didn't want to risk the chance of being slapped again, although I was telling the truth. It did stink undeniably like sweat, funk, and ass.

"Can we still go to the store?" I asked fearing disappointment and losing the opportunity to get some fresh air.

"Sure, kid. Once I bathe and get dressed," he said while continuing on with his reps as if our conversation never took place. He counted silently while breathing slowly in and out, flexed a chiseled upper torso. His white tee shirt drenched in sweat.

Chris was quite the ladies' man. What he couldn't afford to buy flipping burgers at Little Tavern, he got as gifts. Women lingered on his every word while he fed them lie after lie. It was all a game, and he played them one after another. Once he dated two friends, just to see how long he could get away with the charade. Daddy warned Chris that one day his third leg was going to get him in trouble, if his temper didn't get him locked up or killed first. He was good with his hands and was always looking for a victim to punish. Size didn't matter; all he needed was one wrong glance or a few slick words out the mouth. He was angry.

8

Bouncing down the concrete steps and holding on tight to Chris's hand, I almost missed a step as I drank up the sun that licked at my nose, the heat, the humidity, and the strong pungent odor of the honeysuckles in full bloom. It all welcomed me back from the asylum of my room.

Just as we passed the big house on the corner, where the drapes remained drawn no matter what time of day, a woman's voice seductively called out my brother's name. "Hello, Chris. I need you to do me a favor, baby. Would you be a doll and pick me up a few things from the store?"

There she stood, tall and statuesque with glittery hairpins shaped like butterflies adorning her hair, leaning against the screen door, half naked, her body language like that of a cat. She batted long false eyelashes while blowing him kisses through large lips painted with cherry red lipstick, and her pointed nipples pushed through a silk kimono like headlights on a brand new Ford.

"No problem," Chris said. "I was just dropping my little sister off at a neighbor's house. I'll be back in a few."

Chris quickened his pace.

"I'm taking you to Ms. Lola's while I go to the store." he said.

Snatching my hand away from his, standing with my arms crossed, pouting, I asked, "Why can't I go with you?" The words spilled out of trembling lips as my eyes brimmed with tears.

He turned and walked back toward me, bending down close. I could feel his breath on my nose as he sternly spoke through clenched teeth, "Nobody likes a cry baby. If you don't dry up those tears, and I mean fast, I'll never take you anywhere with me again. Do you understand?"

I straightened up, wiping the corner of my eye with the back of my hand before another tear could fall. I wasn't alone in my despair. Just across the street, the new kid on the block sat crying her heart out.

I thought back to when we first met a few months earlier. She had finally mustered up enough nerve, after watching from a distance, to ask if she could join us in a fast-paced game of tag.

"Can I play?" she asked sounding desperate.

"Sure. I'm Amber. What's your name?"

"Chloe," she responded quietly.

"You don't run shit!" Desi yelled as I ducked out of the way. "That dirty bitch can't play with us. She needs a bath. Bet she'd be two shades lighter. You'd need a bottle of bleach to get rid of the ring around the tub." Desi began to laugh as he continued to rag on the young girl. "A straightening comb for that bird's nest." He sounded a little winded as he ran circles around Chloe while snatching a piece of lint from her head.

"Your momma must get a discount at the thrift store. Hope y'all didn't have to stand in line too long for that grandma shit you got on."

Chloe stood defenseless and stunned behind Desi's verbal assault. Those almond-shaped eyes welled up with tears as she turned and ran in the opposite direction.

"You snaggletoothed, pigeon-toed motherfucker, you're so far up Fats's ass that if he farts he'd spit you out," I said.

"You ain't shit! I don't want to play no more!"

"Fuck y'all!" I screamed.

After that, she stopped trying to play with me when the boys were around, and she hardly ever came outside. I wondered if her big brother had hurt her feelings, too.

I struggled to remember her name so that I could speak to her, but I hesitated, not wanting to be wrong. It began with a *c*, that much I remembered. Claudia, Clarissa? No, it was something really different from anybody I knew. Chloe. Yes, that was it—her name was Chloe. I wanted to ask her what was wrong, but Chris was damn near dragging me up the street. My acrylic high heels with the elastic straps scraped the cement. I managed a wave.

My lips stopped trembling by the time we got to Ms. Lola's house. Entering the front door, Fats was seated at the piano practicing for his recital. I cleared my throat, trying to keep from laughing at his chubby ass perched behind the piano. He was proudly wearing his brand new Catholic school uniform: a white short-sleeve shirt, navy blue shorts, and a bow tie with suspenders. He tapped his bare feet on the wooden floor. His dimples were so deep they were almost lost in the folds of his pinchable cheeks. His smile was his pulling card. He loved school and couldn't wait to get back to the elderly nuns that seemed to adore him.

His black ass was constantly reading books, the newspaper, or sometimes even *Life* magazine. He was a smart motherfucker, no doubt. I had to give him that.

Fats glanced up from the keys for a split second to check me out from head to toe as I walked past. I wasn't about to give his ass any ammunition. He joned better than anybody on the block.

Chris squeezed the top of his head as he walked by. "What's up, big man?"

Fats gave him a nod while staring intensely at the music.

"Ms. Lola, you sure you don't mind if Amber stays here for a couple of hours?" Chris asked.

"You know I don't mind, baby," she called out from the kitchen, speaking loudly over water running in the sink and Sara Vaughn's deep sultry voice floating through the air as if riding on a silk cloud.

Tweetie had a big crush on Chris and jumped at the chance to start a conversation.

"Where you going, Chris?" she asked, looking quite uncomfortable sticking out her butt and titties simultaneously just so he'd acknowledge her presence.

I thought to myself, "Look at her hot ass."

"To see a man about a dog," was his response with a sideways smile. All the girls flirted with Chris, no matter what age.

I sure hope the man he had to see about the dog was on the way to the store. He had my money.

"Don't forget my kosher dill pickle, peppermint stick, bubble gum, squirrel nuts—" The door closed shut.

"Damn," I whispered under my breath, "I wasn't finished."

"Come on, let's play jacks," Tweetie said.

"Okay," I replied with a shrewd smirk, thinking, "You 'bout to get your ass whipped!"

"You missed—it's my turn!" I said to Tweetie while sliding the jacks across the hardwood floor, which was badly in need of repair. I struggled to keep all ten jacks in my hand.

Tweetie inquired, "Where is your mommy?"

"In the hospital," I responded.

Tweetie continued to probe. "What's wrong with her?"

"She's got a mental illness."

I let the jacks tumble from my hand and started picking up five at a time, catching the little red ball in between each sequence. Her questioning totally unnerved me, but now I was on a smooth roll.

Ms. Lola spoke from the kitchen, "Hush, child. Somebody might hear you. Gossip spreads like wildfire. Before you know it, the whole block will be flapping their lips."

She sashayed through the archway with a deep bronze tan from a weekend at the beach house. She was wearing a low-cut, tight-fitting black-and-white polka dot dress that emphasized her coke bottle shape and big legs. A Camel cigarette, her favorite brand, dangled from the corner of her mouth. She held a vodka on the rocks in her hand. It was just past noon, and she was getting lit. Ms. Lola sat her drink down, removed the cigarette, and cupped her hand underneath to catch the ashes while her eyes searched the room for an ashtray.

She spoke again. "Don't you never let me catch you two talking about that again." She paused, spotting the ashtray on the fireplace mantel, walked over, and plucked the ashes. She took another drag, deeply inhaling the smoke while she gathered her thoughts. "Everything ain't for everybody. Some things are private, best not discussed. Besides, your ma don't have no mental illness. She's just a bit odd."

That's how it was back then. Mental illness was never discussed, like some strange, hidden taboo.

Listening attentively, the game continued. Tweetie sat across from me Indian style, rolling her eyes and blowing hot air out her mouth with disgust. I'd just breezed through my nines; I was really going to beat her. My eyes were wide with anticipation, and my heart began to race, bouncing the little red ball, just about to clinch the game.

Desi jumped on his bike, pedaling toward us. His back was arched, and his chin was resting on the handlebar. The muscles in his calves were tight like an experienced runner. Rusting metal spokes on rubber wheels squealed out in agony, pushed way beyond their limit. The back tire was semiflat, loping along, slowing down his impending descent as he rode right through the middle of the game. His smile broadened, showing every crooked tooth in his jacked-up mouth, as the jacks hurled through the air like miniature spinning tops.

"Fuck! You curly haired bastard!" I screamed with contempt, jumping to my feet and throwing the red ball at the back of his head.

"Ouch," he squealed like a little bitch as the ball found its mark.

Ms. Lola snatched his ass off the bike with one hand while balancing her drink in the other. The ice cubes drummed against the glass, hopelessly drowning in a wave of liquor. She pinned his bony ass against the wall.

"I've spoken to you before about riding that bike in this house. Let it happen again, and see if I don't give it away. Now take that shit outside to ride." She slapped him on the back of his head with the palm of her hand.

"As for you, little girl," Ms. Lola said, "didn't I tell you the only folks allowed to cuss in this house earned their keep? Last time I checked, your scrawny ass didn't work nowhere."

Fats, still seated at the piano, responded, "Oh, she got a job all right: trying to balance that big head on those pencil legs. Now that takes skill." He snickered at his own joke while glancing over his shoulder in my direction.

I rubbed the tip of my nose slowly with my index finger, staring in his direction, and gave him a silent "fuck you." Displeased with my action, Fats stopped his mockery, his stomach still twitching like jello even though his temperament had turned dark. Pissed with Desi for fucking up my championship game, I wasn't in the mood for Fats's raggin'.

"It's about time for you spoiled brats to have some responsibility in this household," Ms. Lola said as she glanced in the oval mirror checking her lipstick.

"Amber, you write down folks' number bets. Fats, you keep count of the money. Desi, you make sure all windows and doors are locked each and every night."

"Now that I have a job, can I cuss?" I said through questioning eyes.

"You ain't made your first dollar. Don't press your luck, baby girl."

Tweetie went in search of the scattered jacks, crawling on all fours.

"How did Desi and Elena end up living here, anyway?" Tweetie posed the question with her head hidden underneath the curtains and her ass pointed to the sky.

Ms. Lola took a sip from her cocktail before sitting it once again on the mantle. "Elena and Desi lived at the beach house with my friend the judge. You remember meeting him, don't you, Amber?" She continued on with her story before I got a chance to answer.

I'd only seen the Judge a few times that I could remember, tall and strikingly handsome, the movie star type. He could've been Paul Newman's twin with those stark blue eyes.

"Elena was his maid and a damn good cook. I won her in a poker game." A smile ran across her face as if remembering that very night. "Elena, come downstairs."

"Yes, senorita," Elena replied. "What is it that you need?"

"I need you to fill in the blanks where my memory has faded."

Elena took a seat at the table.

"I had no idea that Elena had a little boy. She kept him hidden really well, with the help of my son."

He and Fats quickly became best friends and Fats was sworn to secrecy.

Elena spoke up while folding a basket of laundry, "Desi loved the crazy redhead and her Cuban husband on the television." *I Love Lucy* was the name of the show.

"I like that show. It's funny. Mommy and I used to watch it together," I said with fond memories.

Elena stacked the neatly folded garments to the right side of the basket as she continued on with her story.

"Ms. Lola would sleep in most of the day, and Desi slept when she was awake. All was fine until one morning I went down to the basement to put some clothing in the washer. I remember telling Desi, 'Be perfectly still. I'll be right back.' He looked up at me with those big brown eyes and with the sincerity of an angel and said, 'Yes, Mommy.'

"Desi decided he wanted to imitate his hero, Ricky Ricardo. Handsome devil." Elena's shoulders shook as if she'd caught a chill, lips agape as she sucked in air. We all stared.

"Damn Elena, don't leave a wet spot in my chair." Ms. Lola said in a teasing manner. The two women laughed.

"He ran to the kitchen, pulled out the pots, pans, plastic bowls, and metal spoons from underneath the cabinets. I hear all this racket over my head.

"Oh my God, I almost broke my neck trying to hurdle the mounds of clothing, that same toy box I'd begged the boys to move a thousand times, and the good bike with the bad tire lying on the basement floor. By the time I reached the top step, he was banging away, frantically trying to keep up with the Latin rhythm that runs deep in his soul. Ms. Lola and I almost collided at the landing in the hallway. Ms. L had her pistol cocked. She'd left a trail of pink plastic rollers on the stairway, and her robe was turned inside out."

Ms. Lola joined in with her two cents, as if suddenly her memory was clear, and the story came to life.

Elena screamed, "Please don't shoot. It's my baby." She put herself firmly between the barrel of the gun and her child. "Forgive me for bringing him to your house." Tears were spilling like water from a faucet. "I'll get my things and be gone."

"Shut your trap, woman," Ms. Lola snapped as she put the safety on the revolver, slid the pistol down her side in search of the pocket, and, glancing down, realized the robe was turned inside out.

Desi, entranced with Desi Arnez's performance, kept right on banging those metal spoons against the aluminum pots, oblivious to his audience. The commercial broke his concentration. Turning around, he looked into the eyes of the Forbidden One. He swallowed and stared.

"Bring your little curly haired ass over here," Ms. Lola said.

Desi slowly rose to his feet, grasping the excess material at the waist of the hand-me-down drawers Fats had given him. With his eyes focused on the hardwood floor, he slowly walked in the direction of the shiny satin slippers. He stopped cold in his tracks. The blue silk robe was in plain view. He continued to stare at the floor.

"Little boy, do you realize that you woke me from some damn good sleep?"

EVA S. PINKNEY

"I'm sorry." His words escaped in a whisper from shaky lips.

"Look me in the eye when I'm talking to you. A man looks his enemy square in the eye. Never show fear."

He took a deep breath. Slowly lifting his chin from his chest, his eyes followed the curve of her wide hips, the belt that was pulled tightly around her small waist, and traveled up to what must have been two melons scantily hidden beneath the blue silk robe, until their eyes met. Ms. Lola's harsh disposition melted away when she met the sad brown eyes brimming with tears. Her heart was lost to the young boy with the Gerber baby looks.

"Never say that you're sorry. You're not a sorry person. 'I apologize.' That's what you say. Try not to put yourself in a position where you have to say that too often."

Bending down to his level, Ms. Lola took his face in her hands. Desi's eyes widened as he stared into her gaze and then at the melons.

"Damn, I thought my son was a looker. Don't let pussy be your downfall."

Elena gasped, "Ms. Lola, he's just a boy."

"Not for long in this house. Has the kid got a name?" Ms. Lola asked Elena, never taking her eyes off the child.

"His name is Raul." Elena responded just above a whisper.

"Well after today's performance, we'll call him Desi. Maybe that name will bring him some motherfucking fortune and fame."

Ms. Lola stood up, reached into her bra, pulled out a stack of bills, neatly folded and wrapped with a rubber band. She counted out several one-hundred-dollar bills and handed them to Elena.

"Buy that boy some clothes."

Elena reached out and took the money from Ms. Lola's hand. "I'm forever grateful."

"Show your gratitude by keeping your mouth closed. What happens here stays here. We're family."

Ms. Lola grabbed the handrail to steady herself after bending over to retrieve the hair curlers from the stairs. Now that the adrenaline

52

had stopped pumping, she was reminded of the dull pounding in her head.

"No more white liquor for me." With a look of nostalgia, she said, "Goes down smooth as a baby's ass, but I've got too much Indian in my blood. That shit makes me crazy. I'm going back to bed." Looking back over her shoulder, Ms. Lola said, "And get him some drawers that fit."

We all had a good laugh.

Tweetie and I made our way to the attic for some time away from the boys.

"I'm bored playing dress-up. Let's go downstairs and play doctor and nurse," Tweetie said, stepping out of Ms. Lola's pink cotton dress and throwing it back into the trunk. I scrambled out of the black evening dress with the sequins and followed Tweetie down the stairs.

"What are you doing?" I asked Tweetie as she pulled a key from inside her training bra, turned the lock, and gradually opened the door.

"I watched where Aunt Lola hid the key."

"You know we can't go in there. Ms. Lola will skin us alive if she catches us," I said, backing away while straining my neck at the same time trying to get a peep inside.

Tweetie grabbed me by the hand and pulled me into the sterile room, which smelled heavily of rubbing alcohol.

"Why Ms. Lola got a room like this?" I asked while opening and closing drawers, staring at the white sheets neatly folded in the cabinet and an endless supply of needles and gauze that lined the drawers of the metal cabinet. A stethoscope hung from a coat hook on the back of the door.

"I overheard Momma say she does back-alley abortions down here," Tweetie said while disrobing.

"What's an abortion?" I asked watching her undress. Her breasts were round, mostly nipple. I couldn't wait for mine to begin to sprout.

"It's what you do when you get knocked up and don't want to keep the baby," Tweetie said with a carefree abandon as she removed her shorts. "Take off your clothes."

"Why do I have to take off my clothes?"

"Shhhh. Keep your voice down."

Tweetie reached up and took the stethoscope from behind the door, placing it around her neck.

"Don't you undress when you go to the doctor?" Tweetie said as she stepped out of her cotton drawers. She looked funny standing there butt naked, hands on hips, adorning the stethoscope as if it were a piece of jewelry.

Muffled sounds bounced from wall to wall, lingering in the cracks. Electricity was in the air, ignited by the friction of skin against skin, clit on clit, twisting and turning, inquisitive and naïve. We were playing yet another game: follow the leader. I was a fast learner.

We dressed in silence, nimbly climbing the stairs without being noticed. I took a seat in the parlor, and Tweetie went straight to her room. Solemnly, peering out the window through a blank stare, I was relieved to see Chris come through the front door, even though he'd forgotten my goodies from the store. Somehow I knew what happened between Tweetie and me was wrong, but it felt good in a strange sort of way that I didn't understand, like the tingling in my privates whenever I thought about what we did. I never said a word to anyone.

9

Chloe's knock at the front door was faint but distinct, like a drum roll fading out at the end of a solo. It was almost as if she was afraid the glass would shatter like the fragile pieces of her sad young life.

I peered through the open space in the broken Venetian blind. There she stood with that willowy light brown hair, tangled and uncombed, and faded clothing much too big for her small frame, but her eyes were bright, and her smile was inviting. I'd always been good at reading people, even as a child. Chloe was in search of a friend. I sensed a yearning to be accepted and a need to be protected. Somehow I knew that I should befriend her and, if possible, help her to love herself.

"You want to come inside?"

She nervously glanced down the street and shook her head no.

"Will you get in trouble with your mom?"

"She's dead. My stepmother didn't want me to come live with my father and their family. I hate being there."

My heart went out to her. My mother was sick, but I knew I was loved and wanted.

"Can you come out?"

"Sure. Let me get my jacks and the monopoly game." We spent hours on the front porch, talking, laughing, playing games, and pretending to be the Supremes minus one.

Chloe showed up again the next day and every day thereafter. I gave her some of my old clothing, even though they were still cute, and I took on the job of styling her hair.

"Ouch, Amber! That hurts!"

"Stop being such a crybaby!" I said pushing her forward with a swat of my hand.

"I bet you won't let this shit get tangled up like this no more."

When Chloe turned to look at me she had tears in her eyes.

"Does it hurt that bad?" I asked. "You must be some kind of tender headed."

"It's not that. I need to tell you something, but you can't tell anybody."

"I won't."

"Swear to God."

Raising my right hand in the air I repeated her words, "I swear to God." Little did she know I had my fingers crossed on my left hand, which amounted to an automatic release from my oath of secrecy.

"My stepmother beats me with a razor strap, sometimes a leather belt, until the welts swell and bleed. She never hits me in the face, only places nobody can see."

"Chloe, you have to tell. If you don't, I will."

"No! You swore! Please, Amber. Best friends keep secrets, always. You are my best friend aren't you?" She said it not so much as a question but for reassurance.

"You know I am."

When I closed the front door behind her, my heart felt heavy with the burden of yet another secret.

10

Mommy was still hospitalized under mandatory observation. I wanted to see her. Chris made the call. We pulled onto the sprawling grounds of St. Elizabeth Mental Institution. After being stopped at the front gate by security, we headed to Randall Hall. The building was ancient and under attack by dense crawling ivy that swallowed the dull red bricks whole. We were greeted by the desk clerk, a plump older woman with a kind smile. "We'd like to see Delores Hayden, please," Chris said with his boyish charm.

The clerk smiled adoringly as she handed him the visitor's pass. We took the elevator to the third floor. An orderly unlocked the thick steel door that had two mesh-wired windowpanes. I jumped as the door closed behind us.

My eyes worked double-time scanning the room in search of Mommy. All the patients looked like zombies. The walls were dull, and the ceiling was chipped from an old leak not yet repaired. A strong odor hit my nose: mildew, urine, medicine, and rotting fruit. I spotted her alone in a corner, rocking left to right with her eyes closed, singing "Amazing Grace" loudly and off key. It was one of her favorite spirituals growing up in a Baptist Church. She'd lost so much weight in such a short time that she looked frail.

"Mommy, Mommy." I took off running and jumped straight into her arms.

She smothered me with kisses, putting me down just long enough to kiss Chris and squeeze him tight. I gazed around the room and tried not to stare at the man walking in circles mumbling incoherently.

"Come with me, Mr. Michaels. I'm going to take you back to your room." The male orderly took the man by the arm. Mr. Michaels headed in the direction of his room with that all-too-familiar slow shuffling of his feet. His hospital gown swung open in the back and exposed his flat, wrinkled ass.

A woman with wild eyes and uncontrollable shakes sitting nearby kept screaming in a high-pitched voice, "Somebody get me out of here. Now!"

I played in Mommy's hair, braiding it in two cornrows just like my doll at home. It felt good to see her smile.

Thirty minutes passed too quickly. The orderly announced, "Visiting hours are over." We said our good-byes and watched as Mommy left the room.

"Chris, do we have to go?" I asked.

"I promise you, kid, she'll be coming home soon."

The orderly unlocked the door. Chris followed him out. The woman with the wild eyes jumped to her feet, snatched me from behind, and held me tightly just as the door slammed shut. I kicked and screamed, arms flailing, trying hard to get away, but she was strong. I screamed for my brother.

"Chris, don't leave me!" I could see him through the window-panes, hysterically laughing. I was panic-stricken, and he was laughing. The orderlies were through the door within seconds, and after a brief tussle I was freed from her clutch. I was still shaking when they pulled me from her arms.

Chris asked as we walked in silence to the elevator, "You all right, kid?"

Before I could respond, this asshole was cracking up again. Every time Chris looked at me he'd bust out laughing. He laughed so hard

I began to laugh, too. I was silly like that. We both laughed all the way to the car.

Daddy said laughter was healthy.

Mommy came home several weeks later. Uncle Deke was at the front door, suited down, straight from church. He banged on the door, demanding entrance. He cupped his hands on both sides of his face, pressing his nose against the glass, mouth watering, anxiously peering inside. Uncle Deke always traveled alone, even though he had a wife. She was a little touched, deeply withdrawn and detached from the world. I'd never once seen her leave their house. Today there would be no sad thoughts. We were a family again with Sunday dinners: turkey and giblet gravy, collard greens, potato salad, macaroni and cheese, fresh baked rolls, and sweet potato pie. Mommy had the radio tuned to the gospel station. Chris and I bounced our heads to the beat.

"No dancing at the table," she said with a scowl.

Daddy never looked up from his plate. He knew she had it under control. His woman was home. All was good.

11

Summer of 1965

I was up early, bathed and dressed, and on my way out the front door when I heard Mommy's voice.

"Where are you on your way to, young lady?"

"The record store," I replied.

"I hope you don't think you'll be crossing the avenue by yourself. I can't count the number of people I've seen get hit since we've lived here."

"No, Mommy, I promise."

Little did she know I'd been crossing the avenue for a good little while.

"Don't forget, I got eyes watching you."

"Yes, Mommy, I know." I rolled my eyes and sucked my teeth at the same time, muttering under my breath, "Nosey ass old hussies need to mind their own business instead of reporting my every move."

Today I decided to do as Mommy said. I took all the side streets, navigating my way through well-traveled alleys, making sure to keep my distance opposite the big yard with the German police dog. His head was huge, and he squeezed his snout through every other opening in the massive wire fence, snarling, saliva dripping from sharp canine teeth, barking loudly even after I'd turned the bend.

"Hello, Mrs. Peters. Nice morning for working in the yard. Your lilies sure are pretty."

"How you doing, child?" she said with a wide smile. "I spend a lot of time grooming my babies, but they're worth the hard work and sweat. Where you on your way to so early in the morning?" she asked, removing her gardening glove, opening and closing her fist, wincing just a little as the arthritis settled in more and more each day.

"It's the first of the month—got my allowance. I'm on my way to the record store," I said with a glitter in my eyes.

Now I began to skip. At last, Midnight's Corner Store was in sight, just two more blocks to go.

The record store stood nestled between a barbershop—now under new management—and a clothing boutique.

The bell sounded as I pushed the door open. "Hi, Mr. Sam."

He continued to stack the new arrivals, pricing each album by hand. There were hundreds of albums of every category from Blues to Jazz, classical, and R&B neatly arranged in alphabetical order.

"Hey, Amber." He acknowledged my presence without turning around.

"Mr. Sam, do you have that new Mary Wells?" I stood on my tiptoes and placed the coins on the glass counter full of smudged fingerprints even before receiving an answer.

"Sing it for me, and then I'll tell you if I have it in the back."

Stepping back from the counter with hands on my imaginary hips, eyes shut tight, swaying from side to side like I'd seen Ms. Lola do when she was drunk, I broke into an *a cappella* version of the song.

"Nothing you can do can make me untrue to my guy. I gave my guy my word of honor to be faithful, and I'm gonna. You best be believing I won't be deceiving to my guy."

Mr. Sam applauded my impromptu performance. "Bravo! Bravo, Amber! Let me go in the back and get your forty-five. Girl, you are really something!"

"Is it okay if I take a look at some of your favorite albums?"

"No problem. Use the step stool. No Motown this time."

Mr. Sam was hell-bent on introducing me to all kinds of music. He taught me to listen to the artist no matter what the color of their skin because music has no race or boundaries.

"What've you got there?" he asked.

I carefully handed him an album with four cute white guys with bangs on the cover.

"The Beatles. Good choice. Let me play you a song that I think you just might like."

Placing the needle on the vinyl, he had me with the guitar riff from the jump.

Got a good reason for taking the easy way out

Got a good reason for taking the easy way out, now

She was a day tripper, one way ticket yeah!

It took me so long to find out, and I found out.

I jumped off the stool, moved by the unexpected beat, and broke into a mean version of the jerk, slicing through the air one arm at a time, fists clenched, feeling the music. By the time the song came to an end, I was ready to hear it all over again.

"Here's your forty-five," he said. He handed me the record while walking to the glass counter, where he scooped up the change and placed the coins in my hand.

"This one is on me for the entertainment." His smile was genuine.

"Thank you, Mr. Sam. See you next week."

I scaled the silver wire fence like a trained monkey, my new forty-five tucked safely underneath my left arm, held close to my ribs. The vinyl was wrapped in a thin brown paper bag. I went straight home and wrote all the words down. By the time I knew the song by heart, so did Mommy, who was now singing with me. I could dance before I could walk; I guess I got that straight from my mommy, too, because we played record after record, singing, laughing and dancing the afternoon away, just like old times.

Chris taught me how to hand dance and bop. It was a DC thing. We practiced every day to the latest Motown hits. Berry Gordy was on fire with six hits topping the charts.

"You gotta be smooth, kid. Remember, don't bounce," he'd say while spinning me around. We danced in the exact same spot, directly in front of the stereo, so we could feel the bass.

Mommy fussed, as she squeezed past us carrying laundry, breathing hard and trying to tuck in the extra fifty pounds she'd gained from the medicine.

"You two are going to wear a hole in my rug."

We never missed a beat.

Chris had a new love interest he was trying to impress, so we worked hard. He'd met the young lady Thursday before last on the Milt Grant Show, DC's own American Bandstand. Daddy bought a new television after the old one finally died. He hit the number with Ms. Lola. I overheard Mr. Jackson running his mouth—he couldn't hold water when he was drunk.

I sat right in front of the screen.

"Child, move away from that television before you hurt your eyes," Mommy said.

I scooted back just a little. I was in awe. My big brother was dancing on television. To me, he was star.

Chris had been sneaking girls in the basement for years, but this one was showing up every day, sitting around watching soap operas with Mommy, like she was waiting on her man. She was in love. He was in lust. He wasn't coming home any time soon. He'd found some new tail to chase.

Daddy had warned him, but now he had a bun in the oven. I was in bed, but I heard loud voices coming from downstairs. I crept to the top of the stairs.

"I told your hard head time and time again about them girls!" Daddy yelled, his voice enraged. "It's your senior year in high school. What were you thinking? Now you've got to face up to your responsibilities and be a man. You're going to have to marry this girl and take care of your baby."

I heard Mommy's voice, louder than usual except for when the voices took over with the ranting and ravings of a mad woman. "Chris, do you love her? If you don't, the marriage won't work, plain and simple." She repeated her words. "Do you love her?"

"No, Ma. I don't," Chris replied, his voice shaking.

"Then you'll do the right thing. Take care of your child. There'll be no marriage."

I'd heard enough, and besides my feet were cold. I snuck into my parent's room and pulled a chair up to the dresser. I reached into the top drawer to get a pair of Daddy's dress socks; they were my favorites. My hand touched something smooth and leather, a wallet. I threw it back and kept on feeling around. I felt a small metal object with some sort of material attached. I grabbed it and held it in my hand. It was a medal. I knew my daddy served in World War II. I'd seen a picture of him in his uniform, but I'd never heard him talk about the war. I placed the medal back and continued my search.

I stood on my tiptoes and felt toward the back of the drawer. I felt something cold and metal. I ran my fingers along the barrel, lightly tracing the trigger. Then I heard footsteps. It was Mommy. I snatched a pair of socks, closed the drawer shut, jumped off the chair and hightailed it out of the room. The next time I pulled the chair up to the dresser and opened the top drawer searching for hidden treasure, the gun was gone.

I was up with the sun, standing on the step stool at the kitchen sink and washing my hands. Mommy said you could never be considered a good cook if you weren't a clean cook.

"Wash your hands every time you step away from whatever meal you're preparing."

"If I answer the phone?" I asked inquisitively.

"Especially when touching a surface where so many others have left germs behind," Mommy said. Then she mumbled, "You need to mind your fucking business."

"Mommy, who are you talking to?" I asked fearing the worst. For weeks now the quiet mumblings had begun. I kept it to myself, afraid of losing her again.

"Look, my hands are clean," I said, holding them up so she could see and get her focus back on me. "Can I roll out the dough now?" I'd watched her make all types of pies, cakes, and cobblers, but today I was going to be her assistant.

Drake and Solomon, two rather large black poodles, well behaved for the most part, lay side by side in the hallway. Mommy's employers were away for a few days, so her duties as housekeeper and cook now included dog sitter.

Mommy had just taken the pies from the oven and carefully sat them on the dining room table when I heard Chloe's knock at the front door. Drake and Solomon rose and escorted me to the door.

"Sit down." The dogs responded to Mommy's command, immediately returning to their place of leisure.

"Mommy, I'm going outside to ride my wagon with Chloe."

"I thought you were going to be my assistant today, young lady," Mommy said, never looking back as she proceeded to roll the dough.

"I'll help the next time."

Chloe and I hit the sidewalk after retrieving my little red wagon from underneath the front porch. We took turns pushing and steering, recklessly testing the limit.

"Watch out, mister!" I screamed with a wave of my hand as we neared the bottom of the hill.

Another stranger was descending the steps of Mr. Stone's home. He closed the door as soon as he heard my mouth but not before I glimpsed the wig and silk robe.

Our last conversation turned into a brief shouting match.

"Don't ride that wagon past my property again, you little brat!" he yelled with disgust. "The next time it will be mine."

"My mommy said this sidewalk is public property!" I shouted back. "I can ride up and down this hill as much as I want."

I got the feeling that he didn't care much for kids or women. He wasn't very friendly. He mostly stayed to himself, pruning his roses in his pink button-down shirt, sleeves rolled to the elbows. He wore white khaki shorts, pruning gloves, and a beige straw fedora with a pink band to protect his balding head from the sun. In the evenings, he lounged in his hammock, which hung between two oak trees in his backyard, and listened to classical music.

We'd circled the block enough times that I felt confident about taking off from the top of the hill. The tricky part was maneuvering that corner without flipping the wagon and getting seriously hurt.

"Okay, Chloe. This time, give it a push, get us going, and then jump on."

Chloe followed my directions to the tee. The wagon picked up momentum as we neared the corner. We sat with our backs touching, not knowing what to expect.

"Hold on, Chloe!"

She gripped down hard on both sides of the metal. We took that corner damn near on two wheels, squealing and laughing out of fear mixed with disbelief that we'd actually made it. Chloe dragged her shoes on the sidewalk in an effort to slow us down.

Mr. Stone stepped out from in between the neatly trimmed hedges that lined his vast corner property and surprising us both, snatching us out the wagon. Our bodies swung in midair. My little red wagon came to rest upside down in the grass just shy of the lamppost.

After placing us down on the sidewalk, he walked over to the wagon, picked it up with both hands, and started to climb the steps to his home.

"I told you little hardheads about riding that wagon around this corner. I'm sick of this intolerable ruckus. I can't even hear myself think. I'll just hold on to this for a while to teach you a lesson."

"You can't take my wagon!" I shouted.

"Watch me," he said with an extra switch in his walk.

I'm sure I broke some sort of speed record as I crossed the threshold of our doorway with Chloe on my heels. We were out of breath, and our tears were flying. Solomon and Drake jumped to their feet and barked loudly at all the commotion.

The scent of cinnamon filled the house from the freshly baked apple pies sitting on the dining room table. Mommy was reading the McCall's Magazine. Startled by the front door slamming, my babbling, and the dogs barking, she jumped to her feet and walked toward me in a fast pace.

"What in heaven's name is wrong, Amber?" she asked frantically, already in motion scanning every inch of my body in search of blood.

"Mr. Stone took my wagon," I managed to finally say coherently.

"He did what?" Her eyes went cold and dark.

She turned and walked to the kitchen pantry. Turning the knob, she reached in and snatched the extra door key that was held by blue and orange gimp on the wall hook inside.

Mommy tripped over Drake, who was all under foot.

"Get out of my way, dog!" she yelled. He quickly took a seat at the base of the wooden steps.

Squeezing my hand tightly in hers, she muttered curse words as we turned the corner at the bottom of the hill en route to Mr. Stone's house. I held on to Chloe's shirttail and dragged her along behind us.

"No, that son of a bitch didn't have the audacity to put his fucking hands on these children, much less take my baby's wagon." Red blotches traveled from her chest to her neck, her cheeks, and both ears.

Knock, knock, knock. Mommy pounded on the front door, and the four pieces of carefully placed glass artwork shook. Knock, knock, knock.

"I'm coming! Break those glass panes, and you'll pay for them," Mr. Stone said in a shrill voice.

I barely heard the door break the seal before Mommy pushed her way inside, wrapped her hands around Mr. Stone's long thin neck, and squeezed. She backed him into the corner of the marble foyer as Mr. Stone gasped for air.

"Don't hurt me!" he screamed, visibly shaken and quite surprised.

Mommy scanned the first floor—the white French provincial sofa and loveseat, the curio filled with crystal ornaments, the marble cherub fountain with running water. Beautiful art decorated the walls like I'd only seen on trips to the museum. She loosened her grip just for a second and then squeezed down hard once again.

"Don't ever put your scrawny hands on either one of these children again. Do I make myself clear?" He managed to nod his head yes. "If you forget, I'll come back and force feed your precious roses one by one down your throat. Now get my baby's wagon!"

12

T he bedroom door opened two minutes after I placed the pillow over my face. The sunlight threatened to peel back my eyelids.

"Amber, it's time to get up. Your mother has an appointment at the clinic today. I can't take off work," Daddy said in a rushed voice.

"We gotta catch the bus? Where is Chris?" I questioned as I removed the pillow and squinted at the unwanted invasion of light and warmth pushing its way through the curtains.

"Chris has a job interview today. Now get your butt up. I'm about to leave in a few minutes." Daddy left the bedroom door ajar as he exited.

I made the phone calls to round up the crew. The bus ride to St. Elizabeth's Hospital grounds took two and a half hours, easily, from northwest to southeast DC, including three transfers.

It was hot as five hells on the crowded DC transit bus. The air conditioning was broken, and even with the windows raised high, a wall of people, sitting and standing, wedged together like sardines, blocked the slightest hint of a breeze.

Desi had nerve enough to be flicking that damn lighter. Fats, still holding onto unwanted baby fat, was obviously uncomfortable from the heat. He sweat profusely as he squirmed in his seat, lifted his thigh to unloosen the skin on his legs, which were stuck to the vinyl covering, and constantly wiped the perspiration from his brow. Chloe sat next to Mommy and me, opposite of the two boys, and stole quick glances at Desi every chance she got.

Even the last bus to our destination was crowded. We followed a homeless man—stinking to high heaven—as he cleared a path straight down the middle of the aisle to the back. He was singing a cut off the Temptations' debut album.

"If it's love that you're running from there's no hiding place. You can't run, you can't hide, you can't hide. Don't look back." His voice was strong and more youthful than his battered appearance suggested.

As the bus began to thin out, we quickly claimed the empty seats. I then caught a glimpse of a shorty with an attitude. She was sitting right across the aisle with her face balled up in a knot. Mommy stared blankly, lost in her own private thoughts, and looked right through the young adult.

"What the fuck are you looking at, you old bitch?" the young woman snarled with a rotten tooth in clear view.

I was on my feet and in her face in a split second. "Bitch, that's my mother."

Fats leaned in close, speaking over my shoulder. "Apologize, trick." Fats's voice was deep and intimidating.

No one expected what happened next. The teen stood, ready to take on Fats and me, but Desi cold-clocked her ass from the blind. She fell back into the seat, moaning and clutching her eye.

"This is our stop!" I yelled while holding on tight to Mommy's hand, leading her off the bus.

Fats, Desi, and Chloe ran down the steps, jumping the last three, laughing and giving each other high fives.

We walked right up to the black wrought iron gate and announced to the guard the nature of our business. The air was filled with the smell of fresh cut grass.

"Achoo, achoo, achoo." My allergies kicked in at full speed as I pulled a tissue from my pocket and stopped to blow my nose.

After entering the waiting room of the Thomas Wellington out-patient clinic, I walked up to the desk and signed Mommy's name, saying it out loud as I wrote in third-grade cursive, "Delores Hayden."

"Come with me, Mrs. Hayden," the burly nurse barked, taking Mommy by the arm and leading her down the hallway to the examination room. Her white cotton uniform was wearing thin from excessive starch, and the stocking on her right leg had a huge run starting at the heel and disappearing under the hem of her skirt. Her shoes leaned inward under the weight; they were caked with white polish and squeaked miserably as if calling out for help. Looking back over her shoulder, she said with a distrusting look, "You kids have a seat in the waiting room. Don't touch that channel."

Glancing toward the TV, I recognized the theme music for *The Guiding Light*. Mommy watched channel nine, and I knew that if you didn't want to lose a hand, you resisted any impulse to change the channel, just like the *Lawrence Welk Show*.

"Damn, you think that bitch wanted to be a man? She's got a body like a linebacker," Fats said, settling back into the chair and stroking the few strands of hair on his chin as if he had a full beard.

"She damn sure got the voice to match," Desi said while cracking up. His laughter ended abruptly as he realized Chloe was sitting just a little too close.

"There are about ten empty chairs in here. Find one," Desi said as if addressing a mangy dog.

Chloe hung her head and moved to a seat next to me.

"I don't know why you like that punk. He don't mean nobody no good. You need to quit while you're ahead."

"Sometimes you can't help who you love. I'm drawn to him like a moth to a flame," Chloe said.

"What the hell are you talking about?" I asked, shaking my head. "Never mind. There's Mommy. Let's go."

The next morning, a phone call woke me up. It was the burly nurse from the clinic. She wanted to speak with Daddy.

"Telephone for you, Daddy!"

I came down the stairs in my pajamas and caught the tail end of his conversation with Chris.

A bulging vein ran from Daddy's eyebrow to his hairline, a warning sign that he was pissed. "Your mother slipped out of the doctor's office yesterday without receiving her medication and prescriptions. She's being reassigned to a new psychiatrist. They want to try some new medicine. I've raised hell in the past! She doesn't do well with change. Delores will shut down. I just know it."

Thus began another round of sleepless nights, embarrassing outbursts and the inevitable revolving door between home and St. Elizabeth's.

13

April 1968

Breaking News: Martin Luther King was assassinated in Memphis, Tennessee, today.

Mommy gasped while clutching her chest, as if taking her last breath, followed by uncontrollable tears. Six days of race riots erupted in the city. The smell of smoke hung heavy in the air while businesses were looted and Fourteenth Street burned. Federal Troops and the National Guard were brought in to assist an overwhelmed police force. The city was now under a curfew.

Peering out of the front screen door, I saw two men with bandanas covering half of their faces carrying a black velvet couch with a portable television set resting on the pillows. I ventured out the door and down the steps to get a better view. A frail man with bent shoulders ran right past me with a case of beer in one hand and a lamp tucked under the other arm. Gunshots rang in the distance, and helicopters were circling in the air. Daddy snatched me by the arm, screaming, "Get in the house! Don't you know it's not safe for you outside? You're much too light!"

The next day, Fats, Desi, and I were on our ten-speed bikes coasting down Kansas, to Spring Road, and over to Fourteenth Street. We were too close not to go check out the situation for ourselves. It was like we rode up on a war zone. The GC Murphy was burning out of control. Thick dark smoke billowed from the rooftop. The fire-fighters were working hard to save what was just a shell of a building. A slender man, shirtless with neatly braided cornrows, smashed the window of an electronics store. People scrambled to get inside the store, tripped over each other in haste, and exited with radios, television sets, and stereos. They ran back to their homes before the police could stop them. A large group of angry men approached us from across the street. One yelled out, "What're y'all doing with that half-white bitch?" as he hit a wooden bat against his hand.

"Let's get the fuck out of here," I said, spinning my bike around in the opposite direction. We pedaled as if our lives depended on the quick retreat and rode past the National Guard. Rifles in hand, they were determined to bring calm to a city that was about to implode. I'd finally come to the realization that there was prejudice even among my own people.

Two Months Later

"Desi, get your lazy ass out of that bed, and get that laundry off the line."

I pulled the pillow over my head, trying to block out Elena's yelling, which was in English one minute and Spanish the next.

"I'm coming, woman." Desi sat on the side of the bed with his legs gaped, rubbing his eyes. I caught a glimpse of his penis, heavy with morning piss. He caught me staring, reached down to slowly massage his organ, and grinned as he strolled out of the bedroom. My face turned a shade of crimson.

"Damn, you nasty," I said.

Desi returned minutes later, hollering and cussing. It must have been time for me to get the hell up—wasn't no sleeping happening this Saturday.

This time Fats was awakened by Desi's commotion.

"What the fuck is wrong with you?" Fats mumbled, wiping sleep from his eyes.

"Somebody stole my drawers off the clothesline."

"Why're you so mad? Just buy some more. You got a nice little stash squirreled away." The boys had a very prosperous hustle selling weed to the neighborhood potheads, although I'd heard rumors that they were into so much more.

"What's the problem?" I asked.

"Ms. Lola bought me them drawers. Besides, don't nobody take nothing from me." He'd worked his face into a deep scowl.

"Well, looks like you're ass out today," Fats said. He and I burst into laughter while Desi paced the room in anger.

Early Afternoon

I'd almost forgotten it was the third Saturday of the month; the card game was at our house. Ring, ring, ring. An unanswered phone about to shake right off the hook went unnoticed as I entered the front door. It was just background noise amid loud conversation and an outburst of laughter as Daddy told a joke while pouring another shot. He didn't drink a drop of booze but loved to get everybody else fucked up; he was addicted to watching others act a fool behind the spirit water.

"Hayden, you're a mess," Ms. Walters, from across the alley, said through a flirtatious smile and revealing cleavage. She reached up every other minute to pull on that bird's nest of a wig. Mommy paid her no never mind, because she knew her husband would never look twice at the widower.

A small group of neighbors and friends, nursing a drink or feeding their faces, gathered around eight card tables precariously placed all throughout the first floor. Mommy had set out quite a spread, all for a price. James Brown was on the stereo, desperately pleading with some woman not to go. "Please, please, please." Damn, that man sure knew how to beg, I thought. If she left his black ass after all that, he didn't need her anyway.

Drenched in sweat from the horrid heat, I didn't need to announce that I was home—you could smell me a mile away. I was still high off of conquering Snake Hill on my ten-speed. I backpedaled like a pro, cut through a wall of heat and humidity, held on with one hand, and wiped the sweat from my brow with the other. With each curve more deadly than the previous, I leaned in close over jagged rocks, smartly hidden by green foliage, as they leapt out and threatened to scar me for life. Rounding the bend at the bottom of the hill, I parked my bike against the clay dirt and brick building known as the old Pierce mill. A slight breeze enveloped my face as I walked toward the waterfall. Staring over the edge, I was drawn in by the force of the water, hypnotized.

Fats and Desi had been leaving me day after day, working on some hush-hush project. They were coming home dirty, stinking, too tired to eat, and going straight to bed. I wanted in. They sweat bullets as I approached and saw them feverishly digging a hole in the ground, a brown cloud of dirt covering them from head to toe.

"What the hell are you two fools up to now? Preparing to bury your millions, I would guess?" Laughing out loud, I was greeted with solemn stares from both boys.

Desi was obviously still pissed from this morning's thievery. His jaws were still locked. Fats stopped digging and rested both arms on the wood-handled shovel. He looked blue black, lifted one arm to wipe the sweat from his face, and sniffed his armpit. His tee shirt was drenched with perspiration, and he wrinkled his nose, appalled by his own funk, but he went right back to work.

Desi cast his shovel to the ground, pulled his tee shirt over his head, revealing a deep bronze tan line next to his sun kissed yellow skin, and threw the shirt on the grass nearby. He reached in his back pocket, removed a slightly weathered cigarette butt, and carefully shaped the half-burnt cancer stick before thrusting it between his lips. Feeling deep into his right front pocket, he pulled out his lighter, lit the cigarette, and inhaled deeply.

Picking up the shovel, he continued to dig, finally responding to an almost forgotten question. "We're gonna roast a pig."

"What?" I asked, posing the question with hands on my hips, head tilted to the side, staring at Desi through one slightly shut eye.

"You wanted to be a part of shit," Fats said. "Here's your chance. Think of it as your initiation into the club." Fats stopped digging, staring off into the distance. As if awakened from a daydream, he said, "Go back to my house. Wait outside, out of sight. When the picture man pulls up, stop him before he gets out of the car. Tell him that Desi's hurt. Cry if you have to, but get him here. He'll never hurt Elena again." His bottom lip quivered with emotion.

I turned to look into Desi's eyes, silently questioning the lie he'd told Fats. Desi's stare went cold and blank.

"Yeah, get him here," Desi said. His voice was unearthly, close to a growl.

The three of us stood perfectly still staring into the hole. The only sound was water crashing against the rocks.

I jumped on my bike and pedaled hard, grabbing hold of the tailgate of a pickup truck for a speedy ride up the hill. I knew what I had to do.

Maneuvering through the intoxicated adults, I squeezed between the butt sisters. I barely escaped with my life and left a noticeable perspiration stain on the right and left thighs of the big-boned women helping themselves to second plates of fried fish, mixed greens, and macaroni and cheese. Opening my nostrils wide, I inhaled the fumes but reminded myself there was no time to eat. I only stopped briefly for a glass of water, to show my face, and to grab a fried chicken wing off Daddy's plate. He gave me a wink.

I was really surprised that my parents were entertaining again so soon after the pressure cooker exploded. Chitterlings were dangling from the ceiling like icicles from the roof after a winter snowstorm. It took him hours to clean up that mess, and the smell, phew! More importantly, it was a way to take their minds off the destruction from the riots. People wanted to drink, play cards, and laugh again.

Kissing Mommy on the cheek, I hurriedly announced as I headed for the front door, "I'm staying overnight at Fats's."

"Don't stay up too late, baby. And for God's sake, take a bath before you bless Ms. Lola's sheets," Mommy said, staring intensely at her hand and pondering her next move.

I hated card games and never learned how to play. It was the only time I remembered being ignored.

After ditching my bike in Ms. Lola's backyard, I parked my skinny ass underneath the weeping willow and rested my back against the trunk of the enormous tree. The gentle sway of the green spaghetti string leaves swept against my skin with the tickle of a feathered fan. Totally concealed, I waited.

Thirty minutes or more had passed. I sat cross-legged, still as the dead, and a butterfly came in for a quick landing on my nose just as the white wall tires kissed the curb. Bouncing to my feet, I thought, "The picture man must be drunk the way he bitches and moans about them damn tires."

I pinched myself hard enough to draw tears and ran into the street, waving both hands in the air as I approached the driver's side of the black sedan.

"Desi's hurt. He fell and hit his head." Hysterically crying, I banged my fists on the car door, snot and tears flying as I rambled. He rolled the window down slowly, staring at me through bloodshot eyes and liquor-stained breath.

"Slow down, Lil Bits. What the fuck are you saying?" He leaned his body into the car door, and with much effort, the door finally opened after several failed attempts.

Fats voice echoed in my head, "Don't let him get out of the car."

I ran to the passenger side, jumped in the car, and grasped the sleeve of his usually crisp white button down cotton shirt, which was now wrinkled and stained, to pull his body hard toward me.

"You gotta help. He's not moving. He might die. Hurry. I'll show you where. He's in Rock Creek Park down by the old Pierce mill. Hurry!"

I was engulfed in the scent of yesterday's Old Spice cologne mixed with a hint of bourbon, and the slight contact I received dead on from the joint that was still smoldering in the ashtray made me feel sick. The fragrance found a new home in the pit of my stomach as the picture man pressed down hard on the gas pedal, forcing the sedan to suddenly leap forward. He continued to gun it, leaning with both hands on the steering wheel, staring straight ahead. Watching his every move, I was relieved that his penetrating eyes, which usually fondled my private parts straight through my clothing, were elsewhere.

Beads of sweat ran down the side of his face. His hair began to rise like fresh baked rolls in the oven, new growth for what was usually the perfectly maintained process. That man was known for his manicured hands, bone-straight hair, and the diamond cluster ring on his pinky. His nails were chipped, the ring was missing, and the hair was a definite sign that Ms. Lola was pissed.

Staring out the smoke-stained passenger window, I saw a frail woman with shoulder-length hair wearing a tight red skirt. She melted into a gray brick storefront, which transformed into a DC transit bus. Block after block of blurred images came and went as the black sedan soared up the avenue. The tires begged for mercy as the picture man made a hard left onto Kennedy Street. He soared through each intersection just as the light turned yellow.

A group of young girls jumping double Dutch two at a time darted in and out of the rope, lined up and waiting their turn, each dressed in pink shorts, white tee shirts, and tennis shoes with no socks. Every head was neatly combed in various lengths of ponytails with baby hair outlining their foreheads, and each face shone with a Vaseline glow. The outside world was suddenly clear, and I realized the car was slowing down to a crawl. The dark sedan was drifting slowly into oncoming traffic, the picture man nodding at the wheel.

"Wake up, fool!" Screaming, I grabbed the wheel and brought the car back across the line.

"What? What?" The picture man opened his eyes wide and looked around as if trying to get his bearings.

"Try keeping your eyes open. We're almost there."

Dusk was approaching fast as we pulled into the parking space. He cut on the headlights to illuminate the waterfall.

"There he is!" I said, pointing to the lifeless body. I jumped from the car and ran toward Desi's inert body. "Please be alive."

The picture man stumbled twice on the untied shoelace of his Stacey Adams. The third time, he got a little help. Desi leaped from the ground like a trained gymnast. A flash of silver shone against an orange sun, which was beginning to set. The blade found its mark as Desi turned the piece of steel, thrusting it deeper in the picture man's abdomen.

He gasped for air. The blood traveled upward with a gurgle and spilled from his mouth. Terror and disbelief shone in his eyes as he looked at the three of us. He placed both hands on his stomach, and thick dark blood oozed between his fingers. Removing one hand, he reached up to smooth his processed hair, which was now mixed with blood. Staring back at him and trying to avoid those lifeless eyes, I couldn't help but think, "He was a handsome motherfucker while alive. I guess he wants to be the same in death."

Blood and guts emptied from the wound. Fats walked right up to him. "This is for Elena," he said, pushing the picture man hard in the chest. The blow was just enough to send him flailing backward, like an inexperienced skater, into the freshly dug grave.

The sound of a stalled engine sputtering on a small aircraft circling overhead muffled his cries of death.

Desi sprinted to the back of the mill and returned to the grave, panting for air and holding a gasoline can. He paused, staring down at the man who had violated him, caused him pain, made him hate himself for being alive. Fighting back the tears, he saturated the crumpled body with the liquid. He stopped to remove his bloody shirt. Reaching into his pocket, Desi pulled out a lighter. The flames devoured the cotton like starved hyenas on a fresh kill as he cast the fiery ball into the grave.

"Come on. We've got to go now before somebody sees us!" I said.

Neither boy moved. I turned and bolted toward the black sedan; the engine was still running. Desi and Fats were now on my heels.

Desi climbed behind the steering wheel, Fats got in on the front passenger side, and I dove into the backseat wishing I could sink right through the cushion and disappear. My hands were shaking uncontrollably. The hum of the faulty engine grew louder as the plane's headlights spiraled downward toward the burning grave. Desi threw the car in reverse, peeling out of the parking space backward with his foot pressed to the floor on the gas pedal, just as the plane exploded on impact and burst into flames.

Desi took the sharp dark curves much too fast, awkwardly steering the vehicle, straining to reach the brakes. Fats rode shotgun, massaging the left corner of his bottom lip. We rode through the darkness in silence. Lost in our own thoughts, the events of the evening seemed surreal.

A slippery fart oozed through the cracks of the front seats, damn near cutting off my breath.

"You nasty motherfuckers! Which one of you just bust your ass?"

Desi and Fats looked at each other with that same solemn gaze that I'd experienced earlier. Uncontrollable laughter erupted, breaking the tension.

Rolling the window down, I stuck my head out in search of fresh air. "One of y'all smells like something foul died up in you!"

Desi, still laughing but never taking the charge, reached over and turned on the radio. A popular DJ announced the next song, "This is an oldie but goodie from 1963, Martha and the Vandellas' 'Heat Wave.'"

"Turn that up!" I said, sitting up and leaning forward, resting my chin on the front seat, snapping my fingers, and singing along to words carefully written down and memorized by heart.

Fats's nosey ass opened the glove compartment, searching for anything of interest. "What do we have here?" Fats spoke with the enthusiasm of a child stumbling across unwrapped gifts hidden in the back of the basement closet a week before Christmas.

He examined the weapon from every angle through light brown eyes that shimmered with a child's fascination. My heart fluttered as he pulled back the slide, and the metal clicked as it snapped back in place, the chamber loaded.

Desi was flying as we exited the park, taking a hard right on Upshur, a left on Kansas, and another left onto Ninth. He did a slow roll through every stop sign, made a quick left on Decatur, pulled into a dark alley, and shut off the headlights before bringing the car to rest in an abandoned garage.

As I opened the car door, I hesitated, afraid to place my feet on the ground. A large rat scurried from underneath a discarded dresser onto a pile of trash.

"Fuck this! I'm not getting out of this car. Did you see the size of that rat? Alone, he could swallow me whole." I slammed the car door closed and cast a look at the two of them, leaving no questions.

Fats got out of the car first, tucking the weapon in the small of his back between his sweaty tee shirt and blue jeans. He opened the back door and reached for my hand. His eyes said it all. No words were exchanged. Taking his hand, somehow I knew I would be safe.

"Where are we going?" I asked, fearing the answer.

"Midnight's." Desi said. His eyes were bright like a shiny piece of copper. "Got an itch that needs to be scratched," he said, walking two steps ahead of us.

"I've got to pee." The words escaped my lips with a sense of urgency. Both boys gave me a look of disbelief.

"Swear to God," Desi said, his facial expression changing from a questioning gaze to one of total annoyance.

I fidgeted nervously, crossing and uncrossing my legs. "No joke. I really have to go."

"Squat and pee," Desi said, aggravated. "Fats, let me hold that piece."

Fats handed over the pistol as if it were a half-eaten sandwich. Desi disappeared up the alley.

"What the hell am I supposed to use for tissue?"

Fats reached in his pocket and handed me a red and white bandana.

"Thanks." Apprehensive, I took the bandana from his hand. "Turn the hell around. The last thing I need is an audience."

"Ain't like I never seen it before."

"Stop your lies," I said.

"I guess you've forgotten all those baths we took together as babies," he said.

"You were too young to even know to look. Turn the fuck around!"

Reluctantly, he gave me his back.

I looked around before pulling my white cotton panties, the ones with *Saturday* written in pink across the ass, along with my shorts down to my knees. Squatting, I felt relief as the puddle of water formed between my feet, feeding the dry dirt.

The sound of a gunshot exploding nearby startled me to an upright position. A drop of warm pee ran down my leg, and I swatted it away with the palm of my hand like an unwanted tear as I simultaneously pulled my panties and shorts to my waist, tossing the bandana to the ground.

Desi flew past us on winged feet, like one of the many comic book characters that Chris often read. Fats and I turned and joined in the race. The three of us jumped into the car. The sound of slamming doors echoed off the walls. Backing out of the garage, absent of headlights, we sped away in the dead man's sedan.

We rode for blocks, heading toward Silver Spring, and pulled onto a deserted street just off Blair Road that was filled with abandoned warehouses. Broken glass speckled the tar roadway like hidden diamonds. Spiderwebs hung freely in place of the missing glass panes. Desi wasted no time torching the vehicle.

A pair of white Chuck Taylor's, faded and discarded on a telephone wire, swung above our heads, illuminated by the streetlight, as we dipped into a back alley just off Third and Kennedy Streets. Sam Cooke's "Another Saturday Night" was playing on the radio. The crackle of static mixed with a strong sultry voice, drifting into the air from an open window behind the dilapidated row house on the corner. Fats began to whistle along with the tune unconsciously, a familiar song played often in Ms. L's home. I gave him a hunch to the ribs with my elbow.

"What'd you do that for?" he asked, looking down on me quite agitated.

"Shhhhh." I motioned with a finger to closed lips.

Scurrying like rats along a much traveled pathway, we stayed close to the cement walls and metal fences, away from the dimly lit lamp posts that lined alley after alley. We'd walked several blocks in silence.

"So what happened?" Fats said to a shirtless Desi quite matter-of-factly.

Desi's mouth went into action as if he had been holding his breath far too long and welcomed the release. "I lined those bitches up against the wall and made them drop their jeans to their ankles. I stepped right up to the punk wearing my drawers and splattered his brains against the brick."

"You shot him right there in front of everybody? How stupid can you be?" I said with contempt.

"Now they'll fear me. With fear comes respect." Desi spoke with self-assurance as if someone had appointed him king.

"Fats, you got his back on this?" I questioned, my voice shrill and strained.

Fats answered calmly and directly while pulling a crumpled cigarette pack from his back pocket and lighting up. "As far as I'm concerned, that leaves one less petty motherfucker to worry about and a wide open market for Desi and me to make some real paper."

"But Fats," I said, looking at him with open astonishment. He shot me a look that said the subject was mute. I let him win this round.

We walked again in silence at a quickened pace, avoiding the avenue and slipping into the shadows to escape the nearby sirens.

The night was clear. The three of us lay on our backs, gazed up at the stars, and tried not to trip about our involvement in the horrendous murders committed earlier. Several sets of sheets and blankets heisted from Ms. Lola's linen closet served as a makeshift mattress on the upstairs back porch. Fats lit up a joint as they passed a pint of gin back and forth, taking it straight to the head. Fats was well on his way to becoming an undercover alcoholic. Desi on the other hand, with eyes slightly glazed, displayed his violent temperament.

A slight hint of fish guts neatly wrapped in yesterday's Washington Post trickled just beneath my nose. The fumes managed to push their way to freedom, hitching a ride on a warm summer breeze, from beneath the battered metal garbage can just outside my backyard fence. The waste had turned overly ripe by the sun while awaiting trash pickup on Monday morning. I had the utmost respect for garbagemen, tolerating that funky shit day in and day out. Now I understood why Daddy went out of his way at Christmas to make sure they got an envelope with Franklin's face inside. They deserved that cash along with a few words of appreciation.

Daddy always said, "Acknowledge, respect and help those who are less fortunate than you. You never know what path life has carved out for you. A smile don't cost you nothing." Daddy was a man of few words, but when he did speak his words were memorable.

Stray alley cats clawed in frustration at the metal can wishing for its contents. They climbed on top and licked at a tiny trail of iridescent fish scales scattered about.

"Where is it again, Fats? I can't see it."

"It's right there," Fats said motioning with a nod. Never lifting his head, which was snuggly supported by perfectly positioned feather pillows, he lay with both hands entwined, clasped behind his neck.

"The Big Dipper," I exclaimed. "I can't see it." My bottom lip began to drop, and my eyes filled with water. Frustrated and exhausted from the day's actions, my mind began to race. Two people lost their lives, and I never shed a tear. Now, I was becoming emotional because I couldn't find the Big Dipper.

Fats reached for my chin, slightly tilting it to the left. "It's right there. You see it now?" His hand casually dropped from my chin and tried to cop a feel on my freshly budding breast. I smacked his hand away.

There it was right in front of my eyes. "Wow."

"I guess you couldn't see it with the moonlight bouncing off a mouth full of metal."

"Blinding your ass." Desi flicked his lighter. Open. Close. Open. Close. Laughing, he never took his eyes off the flame.

"You're just jealous. At least I got a daddy to buy me braces. You crooked-toothed fucker, where's your daddy?" I said with a sneer.

"That's why I'm gonna light your ass up as soon as you go to sleep." Desi continued to flick the lighter while moving closer. The flame inched nearer to the leg of my pajamas.

I sat up, drew my knees to my chest, and looked Desi square in the eye. "You forget I live with a crazy woman. I sleep with one eye open." I slid my hand underneath the pillow, flashed the shiny silver blade— one of the pocketknives Daddy used for gutting fish—and pointed the tip at Desi's crotch. "Try that shit if you want. I'll carve you a new set of balls, much smaller, to match that little dick."

Desi's eyes widened. "Bitch, I'm going to fuck you up!" Jumping to his feet, red in the face, and snorting like a bull, he moved in closer.

Fats let out a hearty, deep laugh. His stomach shook with intensity. "Damn, Amber, you know better than to talk about a man's Johnson. Them's fighting words. But at the same time, Desi, you know I can't let you hurt her. She's got too much mouth for her own good, but she's family just like you. Lie down, man. Amber, put the knife away. We've all had a rough day. I swear, I can't figure out why you two just can't get along."

Desi and I exchanged glances of disdain.

"Tonight, I really don't give a fuck. I'm tired. I just want to watch the stars, listen to the crickets sing, and not think about too much of nothing else," Fats said.

"Fats," Ms. Lola summoned with a sense of urgency. "Get down here now. The police want to question you."

ABOUT THE AUTHOR

Eva S. Pinkney began writing as a form of therapy, and she began with poetry before embarking on her first novella. *Crazy Is as Crazy Does: Part One* is based partly on Pinkney's own experiences dealing with her mother's mental illness.

Born in Washington, DC, Pinkney now lives in Camp Springs, Maryland, but she will always be a DC girl at heart. She is currently working on her second book and can be reached at www.talkingparrotmedia.com.

Made in the USA
Middletown, DE
29 July 2017